Penguin Books

BLOOD RIGHTS

Mike Phillips was born in Guyana and came to Britain
in 1955. He has been a teacher, has worked in journalism and broadcasting and is currently a lecturer
in media studies and journalism. *Blood Rights* is the
first of a series of novels about Sam Dean. Mike
Phillips lives and works in London.

Blood Rights

MIKE PHILLIPS

PENGUIN BOOKS

PENGUIN BOOKS

Published by the Penguin Group
Penguin Books Ltd, 27 Wrights Lane, London W8 5TZ, England
Viking Penguin, a division of Penguin Books USA Inc.
375 Hudson Street, New York, New York 10014, USA
Penguin Books Australia Ltd, Ringwood, Victoria, Australia
Penguin Books Canada Ltd, 2801 John Street, Markham, Ontario, Canada L3R 1B4
Penguin Books (NZ) Ltd, 182–190 Wairau Road, Auckland 10, New Zealand

Penguin Books Ltd, Registered Offices: Harmondsworth, Middlesex, England

First published by Michael Joseph 1989
Published in Penguin Books 1990
3 4 5 6 7 8 9 10

Copyright © Mike Phillips, 1989
All rights reserved

Filmset in Palatino

Printed and bound in Great Britain by
Cox & Wyman Ltd, Reading

This book is for my mum, and JC,

and my thanks to Kwesi, JB and Ivor
for their help and ideas

Chapter 1

The doorbell rang just after I had closed the door. That meant
that whoever was ringing had watched me come in and knew
that I was there. I moved to the window and looked out
cautiously while I was wondering what to do. I wasn't expecting
anyone, so it had to be someone I didn't want to see.

Through the slit in the curtains all I could make out was a
smooth blond head. Underneath it was an elegant, grey pin-
striped suit. As I peered out the doorbell rang again, and I
retreated in case he looked up and saw me watching him.

I walked into the kitchen and put the kettle on. I didn't know
anyone who looked like that. It could only be a bill collector. TV,
rent, rates. I could take my pick. But somehow he didn't quite
look the type.

Something stirred in my memory, and I went back to the
window. Just then he looked up and saw me watching him, and
in that instant I recognised him.

He waved with the same nonchalance he'd always cultivated.
Then he pointed and I went down the stairs slowly, wondering
how and why Peter Holmcroft had found his way to my door
after all this time.

We sat on either side of the kitchen table just the way we used
to nearly twenty years before. Pete had produced a bottle of
bourbon, my favourite drink, when I could afford it, and I was
surprised that he'd remembered after all this time.

But when I thought about it, it wasn't all that surprising. We had shared a flat as students, and there was a sense in which the years in between had somehow disappeared as we sat there. This was Pete, who I had known, for a time, as well as I was ever to know anyone.

'Well,' he said, raising his glass. 'Here we are again. What's going on?'

I shrugged. I was broke. I knew a lot of people, but I didn't like any of them very much. There was little to tell.

'I keep reading your articles,' Pete said. 'You're famous.' He grinned, creating a short pause. 'In a very small way.'

I was familiar with this game too. We'd have to insult each other for a little while at least.

'The last time we were together, you were dressed in a pair of greasy jeans and an extremely smelly T-shirt, planning boring ways of embarrassing your family. What happened?'

What had happened was that he now looked very prosperous. The grey suit looked as if it had been made for him. His fair hair was styled and every time he moved I caught a whiff of some pricy aftershave.

'You look like a right dolly,' I said. 'What are you doing now?'

He laughed. His look became a little sly, as it always had when he was about to pull some kind of stroke.

'I work for an MP,' he said. 'Grenville Baker.'

I nodded. I knew about Baker. He wasn't just an MP. He was one of those who'd become natural heirs to power. Connected by birth to a couple of powerful political families, he had inherited old money and become a figure in the electronics industry before going into Parliament. For the last year or so he'd been talked of as a future Cabinet member, and he was already a regular on the TV talk shows. If he was going places, it was clear that Pete was going with him.

'I heard you'd joined the Conservatives,' I said.

This was putting it mildly. He'd become a minor guru of the New Right, a fact which had made me laugh when I first heard it, because Pete had made a fetish of not opening a book while he was a student. He'd recently written one though, on the death of the Welfare State. He gave me the sly look again. It made his blue eyes look slightly crossed.

'Well you couldn't see me joining Labour, could you? Trying to conceal my origins and spending my evenings at meetings with the kind of objectionable shits who used to infest the students' union?'

He had talked like this in those days too. I'd talked like that myself. For different reasons, of course, but it was the same crap.

'Mind you,' he said, laying his finger to the side of his nose. 'It's done me no harm having gone to a gritty university like London. Makes me an intellectual, especially when they find out I lived for years with a black man. That doesn't go down so well with the troops, but the bosses find it interesting.'

His cynicism began to depress me. In our student days it had been an amusing pose which he used as a shield. Now it was a way of life.

'Cut the bullshit,' I said. 'Is this a social visit or what?'

'Well, I did want a small favour.'

'Ah hah,' I said. 'What can I do for you?'

For a moment I thought I knew what it might be. A surprising number of people imagined that I could write flattering profiles about them. I couldn't, but it was a common mistake.

Pete took a swallow and set his glass down firmly. He stared me straight in the eye with a sincere and intense blue gaze which he must have learned in some school for aspiring politicians.

'It's not for me exactly. Baker's got a little personal problem with which you might be able to help.'

I frowned. This was becoming weirder and weirder. I could just about imagine Pete needing a favour from me, but Baker had as much to do with my life as the jet plane I could hear passing overhead.

'You're not giving me a preview of the next scandal, are you? What is it? Sex, drugs or thieving?'

Pete gave the comment a small smile. 'It's his daughter, Virginia. She's a student, and in the last couple of weeks, she's disappeared.'

'Disappeared?'

I knew about Virginia too. She appeared from time to time in the gossip columns as one of the crowd at some dance or club. They always described her as the 'daughter of the prominent MP'. I'd seen a picture of her on stage at a fashion show for charity and another on the arm of a pop musician. She was a

3

slim blonde, not pretty, not plain, who I wouldn't have recognised from the smudgy newspaper prints.

'She shares a flat with friends in Notting Hill. She hasn't been there for a while, and her parents are worried.'

'I didn't know parents like them worried about not seeing their kids for a few days,' I said. 'Isn't disappeared a bit strong?'

'Difficult.'

He considered. His expression changed, the professional frankness vanishing. His eyes brooded.

'She usually keeps in touch.'

'Why don't they try the police?' I knew the answer to that. You can call them in, but you can't call them out again. Most of the time.

'Come off it. The police won't actually go out looking and in any case she might turn up tomorrow.' He paused. 'And, no one knows what's going on, of course, but the circumstances might just possibly require discretion.'

'No scandal, eh?'

'A scandal's unlikely,' he said. 'But we'd rather not attract any more attention than necessary. All they need is to locate her and be sure she's all right. You know what kids are. She'll probably turn up, astonished that anyone noticed anything.'

'So why bother?'

'They're parents and they're worried. I'd find her myself. But we've got a conference coming up and a possible Cabinet reshuffle. I'm up to my neck in it. In the circumstances . . .' He cocked an eyebrow at me and let the sentence trail off.

'In the circumstances you all want to make sure that there's nothing nasty happening which the bosses might get a whiff of. Just at this crucial juncture.'

Pete's smile was positively frosty.

'Baker simply wants to make sure that she's all right.'

'So why me? I mean I appreciate you thinking of me, man. But I'm a journalist, and I'm black. Sure as hell Baker doesn't want me fooling around with his daughter.'

'All this is confidential,' Pete said quickly.

'Pete. Who cares if some second-class Sloane Ranger ducks out of college? You think I'm going to flog that to Nigel Dempster?'

4

Pete laughed. 'Same old Sammy.'

'Never mind the flannel, old cock. Why me?'

He smiled, rested his elbows on the table and put his clasped fists in front of his mouth, with his chin supported by his thumbs. Then he took them away, leaned forward and gave me the intense look. He compressed his lips, screwed his mouth up, and raised his eyebrows. His expression said that he was going to be frank.

'Well. That's just it you see. You're the only black person I know well enough to trust.'

'What's that got to do with it?'

'Everything, I suppose. She's been chums lately with a young black man. It's possible that she's with him. That might be it.'

'Complicated.'

'Yes.'

'Drugs?'

Pete sighed. 'It's probably better if you talk to Baker about all this.' He took out a card and scribbled on it. 'Here's his address. If you're interested he'll be at home this evening, and he'll expect you for dinner.'

He reached over and put the card on the table in front of me. I didn't move.

'This is ridiculous, Pete. Being black doesn't actually qualify me for locating people, even if there is a black youth involved. I'm kind of intrigued, but I'm not interested, you know.'

'Do me a favour, Sam. As a friend. Go and talk to him. He really wants you to.'

'But why, Pete? Why me? The guy doesn't know me from Adam.'

'He's read you. That's how we both thought of it. A few months ago we were reading an article of yours in the *Guardian* and I said I knew you. Yesterday he asked me about you. I said if you agreed you'd keep quiet about it.'

I grimaced.

'What have you got to lose?' he said. 'You're a freelance. You're accustomed to looking up facts and all that. What's the difference? He'll pay you.'

I picked up the card and looked at the address.

'Go and see him,' Pete said. He poured me another shot of bourbon and winked. 'Okay?'

I nodded. He was right. I had nothing to lose, and I was curious.

'Okay,' I said. 'I'll go.'

I thought he looked a little surprised. Perhaps he'd been prepared to do a lot more persuading. Perhaps he'd been prepared for me to show him the door. But he'd caught me in one of those moments when the only job I had on hand was to count my last pennies.

Work didn't come easy for a black man in my trade, and I was twisting slowly in the wind. Any likely proposition would have caught my interest, but everything that Pete had said hinted at a secret drama that made my instincts twitch.

Whatever it was had been dropped in my lap like a gift-wrapped package, and I couldn't resist the urge to open it up.

'I'll tell him then,' Pete said.

'Don't worry,' I repeated. 'I'm on my way.'

Chapter 2

Baker lived across the river in South London. Around seven in the evening Wandsworth Road was still jammed with traffic, and I crawled along in it until I'd got past the polytechnic and I could turn off.

I'd come across Chelsea Bridge and driven along the river up to the Archbishop's Palace. It was one of my favourite places, partly because whenever I drove that way I remembered approaching Lambeth and seeing a rainbow hanging above the river, just past the bridge. My son had been in the back, and I still got a kick out of recalling his excitement.

There was no rainbow on the day that I first went to see Baker, but it was one of those warm summer evenings when the city trees were suddenly shiny and green, and the sun danced on the river, and even through the blue petrol haze, London looked beautiful and strange, as I imagined a tourist might see it.

Off Wandsworth Road the traffic was so thin it was hard to imagine that the honking press of vehicles I'd just left was only a hundred yards or so away.

Baker's house was reached through a maze of short streets, crescents and squares. As I parked on the end of his crescent a vagrant memory struck me. During the nineteenth century Engels wrote that the houses and shops of the rich lined the main streets of Manchester, while the people who worked for them were hidden behind the barricade of wealth.

We lived now in subtler times. Busy streets like Wandsworth Road were lined with council flats, while behind them nestled older houses, restored, gentrified and expensive.

As I rang the doorbell I looked around the square. When my family arrived in London more than twenty years before, we'd lived in a little street like this, in a house exactly like Baker's. But in our house a different family lived on every floor and we thought of it as a crumbling slum. All through my boyhood I had longed to get away from houses like this and live in a neat suburban box smelling of new paint and varnish.

For a moment I wondered whether Baker would appreciate the irony, and I was still smiling at the thought when he opened the door.

'Ah,' he said. 'You're Samson Dean. Grenville Baker.' He put out his hand and shook mine firmly. 'Very good of you to come. No problems getting here?'

While he ushered me in he told me that his friends had difficulty finding where he lived. I studied him covertly. He had very nice manners, and although his geniality might have been only skin deep, his reception made me feel welcome, almost relaxed.

He was wearing a cashmere sweater with an open-necked white shirt. I knew he was in his mid forties but there was something youthful about him, as if he were just about to slip into cricket whites and go out to bat for the school.

The room we went into was large, the depth of the house, with bow windows looking on to the crescent, and, on the other side, open french windows through which I could see a neat lawn, bordered by rosebeds.

Baker's wife was sitting in one of the two sofas in the room. She was wearing loose white slacks through which I could discern the shape of her rounded tapering thighs. Her hair was only a little darker than his, and her eyes were a slightly warmer shade of blue, but she had the same deceptively youthful air, and the same diffident politeness.

'My wife, Tess Baker,' he murmured, as we shook hands.

I sat down, and she got up to get me a drink. I said I wanted whisky. As she went to the corner of the room, I was struck by how much they resembled each other. They might have been brother and sister. Oddly, Pete resembled them too, and I wondered whether Baker had deliberately chosen an assistant who had the same colouring.

I had been staring at the line of watercolours on the wall facing me, and Baker followed my gaze, smiling. He nodded at the pictures.

'They're nice aren't they? My wife collects watercolours.'

'Oh I got most of them years ago,' she said, coming back and handing me a glass.

They were Victorian, I guessed; and they were the sort of pictures now fetching tidy sums at auctions. But I was ready to bet she had inherited or been given them.

'I could hardly afford to collect them now.'

I'd heard that story before. The world was full of things that people like the Bakers couldn't afford.

She sat down again, smiling at me in an oddly companionable way. If the two of them were under pressure, as I was sure they were, they showed very little sign of strain. As the sun faded they chatted amiably as if I were just another guest who'd dropped in for the afternoon.

Baker had done his homework. He mentioned an article I'd written about Jamaica and began talking about the Caribbean and Latin America.

US policy, he agreed, was ineffective or misconceived. Tess Baker nodded, and told a story about Brazil. She was connected with a merchant bank, and she'd visited a conference there a few years ago.

Even then, she said, it had been obvious that the World Bank and the IMF would fail to provide answers to the problems of development.

Both of them had the politician's trick of appearing to solicit your opinion, appearing to listen carefully, and then delivering their own views, no matter what you said.

In a short while she got up and went out. I presumed that she'd gone to the kitchen. Baker continued talking, about my articles, about England's prospects in the Test, about anything apart from the real business of my visit. I didn't push it. They had gone to great pains to treat me as a social equal, and Pete would have advised them about how to handle me. But my suspicion was that under the cultivated chatter Baker was embarrassed.

In fifteen minutes or so we followed her. The pine refectory table was laid for three, with two bowls of salad in the middle. We were having grilled pork chops and new potatoes, and the Bakers tucked into the meal with gusto. The upper and middle classes in England still loved to eat like schoolkids. Sausages, peas, bacon, chops, puddings. Like cheese to a mouse.

We were halfway through the meal before Baker raised the subject.

'It's a small problem,' he said, 'but we could use your help.'

'Why me? I would have thought that you'd have a number of alternatives.'

'That is the problem in a way. It may be that Virginia thinks we wouldn't approve of her friendship with this young chap. If she felt we were being heavy-handed parents, sending the police after her, that sort of thing, it might simply make matters worse.'

'Why don't you just wait till she comes back?'

'Well. Yes. There it is. The point is that we don't quite know what's happening. We just want to know where she is.'

'Couldn't you try a private detective?'

Baker smiled wryly, and looked at his wife. 'That's not an option we feel very happy about,' he said.

He leaned forward.

'Look. It's something that we'd ask a family friend to do. We tried various members of the family, in fact, to see whether she'd gone off to my father-in-law's farm or any of the other homes. One of my nephews looked around the discos. But when this business of the black boy came up we didn't quite know how to manage that aspect.'

'Not something we could manage in the family,' Tess Baker said. There was a slight edge to her voice, and Baker looked at her quickly.

'Are you happy about me doing it?'

'Peter has great respect for you,' he said seriously, 'and I trust his judgement, especially now we've met you and talked to you. He said it was something that you could do easily. He also said that you weren't interested in personal gossip.'

He was right about that at least. I wasn't the kind of journalist who found minor personal secrets exciting, and I'd always felt that the gossip columnist's trade was more or less disgusting.

Pete must have remembered me going on about it. In any case none of this was quite interesting or important enough to make headlines.

'Peter was sure you could help,' Tess Baker said. She smiled at me with something tremulous in her expression and when I looked at her she dropped her eyes to the table.

'I can't promise,' I said. 'But I'll think about it.'

'Oh, well done,' Baker said.

They were looking at me expectantly.

'Has she ever done something like this before? Dropped out of sight, I mean.'

'No, she hasn't,' Mrs Baker said. 'That's just why we're worried.'

'What about this black youth? Who is he?'

'I don't know,' she said. 'I went to try and see her at the flat last week, and I asked her flatmates whether they'd heard from her. They said they hadn't, then they told me that this boy had come to visit her a number of times in the last month. They didn't know him and she didn't introduce him. They just shut themselves in her room.'

'Perhaps I can talk to them,' I said. 'If I said I was writing about you it won't surprise anyone that I'm asking questions.'

'Yes,' Baker said. 'That's a useful idea.'

He glanced at his wife. She reached back to the sideboard behind her and when she turned round again she had an envelope in her hand. She put it on the table in front of me. Her big round breasts moved around in her shirt as she did this, and I tried not to look at them.

'There's a photograph of her in there, and some addresses you might find useful.'

I opened the envelope. The photo showed a grinning teenager. I'd been with her parents long enough now to sort out the differences in their features, and I could see that she had broad, high cheekbones and wide-set round eyes, like her mother. Clipped to the photo was a sheet of paper on which was typed a list of names and addresses.

As I was about to shove it all back in the envelope I noticed a third piece of paper. It was a cheque made out by Tess Baker for £500.

I looked up. Baker got up and started taking the plates away, divorcing himself from the conversation. Tess looked straight back at me, but now there was something unreadable, aloof, about her gaze.

'Expenses?'

I waved the cheque a little.

'They tell me journalists can't function without them,' she said.

She smiled. I shrugged. The cheque made me an employee.

'I'll see how it goes,' I said.

Her eyebrows shot up, but I simply stared back at her, letting the issue hang in the air.

Baker broke the silence by clearing his throat. 'If you let me know, or Tess of course, as soon as you can locate her.' He had rejoined the land of the living now the money bit was over. 'We can go and see her as soon as we know.'

'I can't promise too much,' I said. 'She may not even be with him.'

'Well. If we knew that much it would be some sort of progress.'

He smiled and ducked his head sideways in a wry gesture. I got up and said goodbye to Tess Baker. She stood up too. Close to her, I noticed, for more or less the first time, how tall she was, only a few inches shorter than me. I wondered about her age. She was certainly in her late thirties, probably over forty. She had crow's-feet creeping into the corners of her eyes, but her clear, smooth skin and her firm rich body made her attractive.

'Good luck,' she said, as she shook my hand, but her tone and her impassive look made me think that the wish was for herself.

Baker ushered me, almost ceremoniously, to the door. I wondered whether he would urge discretion on me, but he merely told me it would be easier getting back across the river now the traffic was thinner. At this time of night, he said, he could make it to the House in less than fifteen minutes. I told him that must be convenient and said goodbye.

I looked back as I got to the car and he was still watching me from the doorway. Framed in the light, he looked a powerful and confident figure, but the way he stood made me think of a stage in which he was part of the scene, an actor playing a role. As I found my keys he closed the door and the set vanished as if a curtain had come down.

I drove back along Wandsworth Road thinking about the evening.

On the face of it the matter was simple. They could handle a conventionally wayward daughter. But the addition of the black youth to the scene, together with her dropping out of sight, had changed the pattern and made them uneasy.

Something about Baker's manner when we stood at the door had told me he was seriously worried.

At first I'd thought that it was merely his horror at having exposed their domestic secrets, but Baker knew as well as I did that London was full of journalists who knew discreditable things about politicians and wouldn't or couldn't print them.

That wasn't it. It was their daughter.

When I'd put the photo away the Bakers' eyes had clung to it as if that were the last they'd see of her.

As I turned left at the river I caught a glimpse of Big Ben, and it reminded me of a Conservative Minister I had interviewed in his room at the Commons. He had been much older than Baker, but he'd been the same height and had the same laid-back attentiveness. He'd answered all my questions in courteous detail and when I left he shook my hand powerfully, towering above me.

'Go back,' he said, to my astonishment. 'Go back and tell your people that we bear them nothing but good will.'

For a moment I almost replied, 'Yes bwana.' But that was the kind of joke I had learned might blow the whole story.

Besides, there was something touchingly transparent about the old imperialist. Baker was harder to read and that worried me. I was sure that I'd only seen the tip of the iceberg, and that I might be letting myself in for something that would damage me.

Back in the flat, I turned on the TV and sat in front of it going over the story they'd told me. The programme was one of those late night conversations in which three people sat around using long, difficult words and looking pleased with themselves. After a while I gave up trying to work out what it was about and changed channels. A golf match came on to the screen. I turned the sound down and let my eyes rest on the soft green landscape.

Just before I went to sleep I wondered whether the Bakers were watching this and dismissed the thought. That pair would be out doing something useful.

Chapter 3

Disaster struck the next morning.

The following week might have gone differently if the buff envelope hadn't dropped through my letter box just as I was getting up.

I'd begun to have my doubts about the Bakers' business, and some time during the night I had decided that if I changed my mind I could always send their money back and wash my hands of the whole affair.

The bank manager's letter closed off that avenue of escape.

He said, in language like a cold flat stare, that I had to deposit enough money to cover three cheques that I'd paid out recently, or they would be dishonoured. My overdraft, he continued, was well over the limit we'd arranged, and he would have to see me to discuss my position.

I crumpled the letter up and threw it into a corner of the kitchen, then picked it up again and smoothed it out.

This was real trouble. My last job had netted me enough to pay off the previous overdraft so I'd been reckless and paid the bills on the strength of it. But it hadn't been enough to stop the bank losing patience.

I took a deep breath and sat down to think it through.

I had a couple of articles to deliver but the deadlines were several days away. I hadn't any hope of getting paid for another month. Over the last year I had borrowed more than I should from too many people, and it would be painful and perhaps pointless doing the rounds again.

The Bakers' cheque was my only resource. But using it would tie my hands and commit me to doing what they wanted. I hadn't thought of it in that way before, and at the back of my mind I felt a small tickle of resentment at the idea.

I ran my eye down the letter again, casting around for alternatives, but halfway through I knew that the decision had been made.

I got the cheque out and laid it on the table next to the bank's letter. Then I went into the next room and rang Pete's office.

He recognised my voice right away.

'Samson. You went to see him.'

'Yep.'

'That's great.'

Passing the problem over to me must have meant that he'd got Baker off his back.

'Tell me something about the girl, Pete. I didn't want to ask her parents. They probably think she's purity itself.'

'Oh I think they're a little more realistic than that. Baker's one of the few who keeps in touch.'

I interrupted his sales pitch.

'Even so.'

'Yes. Well. What do you want to know?'

'What kind of girl is she? Has she done this before? Does she screw around a lot? Is she bright or a dummy? Is she into dope?'

There was a moment of silence on the line.

'I don't know that much about her,' Pete said cautiously. 'I can tell you that she only left school a couple of years ago. She's just twenty. She seems a serious person. I mean she could have done a number of things but she insisted on going to college. I don't know much about her friends but they seem the usual bunch.'

'What about dope?'

'I don't know. I don't suppose she's any more into dope than we used to be.'

'Any special boyfriends?'

'I don't know.'

'Does she go?'

'Come on, Sammy. How would I know? I'm a happily

married man nearing middle age. I'm not that interested. You dig?'

The phrase reminded me of how he used to be. I laughed sceptically. 'Bullshit, Pete.'

I put the phone down. Later it might be worth talking to Pete again, but I didn't yet know the right questions to ask.

Chapter 4

Virginia's college was in the centre of London with the main entrance in a backstreet, where small knots of students stood around talking. They looked more or less the same as they used to in my day. No matter how profound the changes in fashion and style, students seemed to continue looking the same, except that they got younger.

On the other hand, everyone was getting younger.

I told the man at the reception desk that I had an appointment with the college secretary and went on up to the first floor office where he directed me.

'I've got a message for Virginia Baker,' I said.

'Baker?' She thought for a moment, not looking up from the chart on which she was working. 'Why don't you put it in her pigeon hole?'

'Pigeon hole?'

She looked up, and took her glasses off. She was pale and freckly, with green eyes and carroty hair.

'Yes. You know what a pigeon hole is, honey. I can tell.' She grinned. 'That's how they get messages from the outside world. Go up to the canteen and you'll see a stack of them with initials on each one. You put your message in there.'

I smiled at her. She had a cynical, perky manner that I liked.

'You can read me like a book,' I said, 'but the thing is, this message is from her dad and he asked me to see her personally and put it in her hands.'

Before I got out of the car, I had slipped a piece of blank paper into an envelope. I waved it.

'He wants to make sure she gets it.'

'Virginia Baker?' She frowned, remembering. 'Oh yes. Her parents have been ringing up, but we haven't seen her.'

She paused to look at me with her chin resting on her fist.

'Why don't you go and see George Evans? He's her tutor.' She looked at a wall chart next to her desk. 'It's gone twelve, he should be free.'

She picked up the phone and dialled.

'George? There's a man here from Virginia Baker's parents. He's got a message. He wants to see you.'

She put the phone down and gave me George Evans's room number. I thanked her and in an almost involuntary gesture I winked at her.

She smiled, as if to herself, and swung back to her desk.

'You don't really mean that,' she said, immediately looking away and lifting her pen to start work on her papers.

I shut the door quietly behind me, and climbed the nearest flight of stairs to the tutor's room.

'Come in,' a voice said sharply from behind the door when I knocked on it.

I opened it and hesitated because the room was so small, half filled by the desk at which George Evans was sitting with his back to me. As he looked around I got the impression of a round face, rimless glasses and greying hair. I waved my message at him, and he looked sceptical. He had a serious expression which was at the same time bland and boyish, like a TV weatherman.

'You're from Virginia's parents?' he asked.

'That's right,' I said. 'They did want me to see her.'

'That's odd,' he said. 'We haven't seen her in classes for a while, but her brother rang a few days ago and said she was ill.'

'Her brother,' I repeated.

'Her brother Roy,' he said impatiently. 'I expect she's having a little holiday. If you see her can you ask her to ring me?'

I nodded. He said goodbye with a grunt and turned his back on me. I went back down to the lobby. The pay phones were engaged and I went back up to the secretary's office.

'Sorry to bother you again,' I said. 'But can you tell me which class she's in?'

19

'Film and Photography two,' she said. She gave me an exaggerated wink and I closed the door fast on her.

I went down to the canteen where the students were queueing at a counter. I spoke to the girl at the end of the queue.

'Are you in Film and Photography two?'

She looked at me almost with alarm and mumbled a 'no'; I looked round for someone who wouldn't panic about talking to a stranger.

'Who are you looking for?'

I looked round. The woman who had spoken was older than most of the students in the canteen, in her mid twenties at least. Her green eyes were nearly on a level with mine, just short of six feet, and she had wide shoulders, black hair and a golden olive skin.

I must have goggled at her like an idiot, because she frowned a little and repeated her question.

She had an accent I couldn't place. In the USA I'd have said she was from Puerto Rico or Cuba, but in London I couldn't decide.

But I knew one thing. I had to find out.

'Can I buy you a coffee?' I said.

'Ten minutes. I'm in the middle of a lecture.'

We sat together in a corner, and I told her about my message. She pursed her lips and frowned.

'She's not exactly a regular attender. She wasn't bad the first year, but lately she hasn't been around much. Have you tried her flat?'

I ignored the question. I didn't want to lie to her and I didn't want to go into why I was asking the questions. I just hoped she'd keep on talking. The longer I was with her the warmer her eyes looked. They were an odd green and they had hazel flecks in them. She had to be Spanish, I thought, but I'd never seen a Spaniard who looked like her.

'She's not interested in her studies?'

'No.' She paused. 'I don't know. I don't really know her very well. She's different.'

'What do you mean?'

'Well she's got her own car, her own flat. She lives differently. She's kind of a social star. You know? Goes to discos. A lot.'

Her lips took a wry twist on the last sentence.

'I thought all you students did that.'

She smiled widely, as if she thought I was being provocative. 'Maybe all students who can afford it. Students' grants don't go that far nowadays. Most of them spend their time worrying about the rent or about finding a place to live.'

'Virginia's got no worries?'

'Her father owns the flat she lives in. It's a great place. I took some photos of her there.'

I twigged at last.

'You're not a student.'

She laughed. 'No, I'm a photographer. I teach here part-time.'

'Sorry.'

'Don't be. It's quite flattering, I suppose.'

'I didn't set out to flatter you,' I said. 'If I had I could have thought of several much more obvious things.'

One of my cuter lines.

'That's as maybe,' she said. 'But my time's up.'

She put her cup down and pushed her chair back.

'Wait a minute,' I said. 'Is there anything more you can tell me?'

She shrugged and waggled her head slowly. She looked nice doing it.

'When I was there they were talking about going to the country for the weekend. Someone said they'd be high for days and they all laughed.'

'Into dope?'

She shrugged. She looked nice doing that too.

'Perhaps. I don't know. You know what that sort of kid is like. They giggle a lot without telling you the joke. I didn't want to know anyway.'

'Would she have any boyfriends or special friends in here?'

'No. She doesn't have a lot of close friends here. Why are you asking all this anyway?'

I shrugged.

'I'm just trying to contact her.'

She raised her eyebrows at me and got up abruptly.

'I've got to go.'

'Thanks a lot,' I said, then I took a deep breath. 'Tell me to get lost if you think I'm being too personal but where are you from?'

She considered me gravely for a second.

'Get lost,' she said.

We stared at each other. I knew it was only my imagination, but the canteen seemed to have gone silent.

'I'm sorry,' she said. 'I wanted to see what you would do.'

I shrugged. All I could think was that in a moment this creature would disappear, and I'd never see her again.

'Do you want to talk about it later?'

She smiled down at me, but for a moment I thought about saying no.

'Yes,' I said.

'Five o'clock here. Okay?'

She left, moving fast. As I watched her back going out of the door I realised that she still hadn't told me anything about herself, and it struck me that, in much the same way, she might know a lot about Virginia and her friends that she wasn't telling me.

I looked around. Two tall girls paused by the table. One of them had mauve-coloured hair, the other strawberry, and they were both dressed in black, with long spindly legs covered by wrinkled black tights. I smiled at them so as to be doing something with my face, but when I did that they sheered away as if my expression signalled hostility.

Alien turf. I got up and left, and at the foot of the stairs I found myself looking for the woman in the crowd of students going up and down. But she'd vanished, and, feeling a little foolish, I made my way up to the pay phone in the lobby.

I rang Pete's office and he picked the phone up immediately.

'Pete. One more question.'

'Make it quick.'

'Has Virginia got any brothers?'

'Yes. Two. They're away at school at the moment.'

'How old are they?'

'Nine and eleven.'

'Names?'

'James and Douglas. What's this all about, for God's sake?'

'Talk to you later.'

I put the phone down. The brother Evans mentioned must have been a friend trying to get her off the hook. Perhaps one of her flatmates.

I took out the list of addresses Tess Baker had given me.

Virginia's flat was in Kensington. Going there had to be my next step, but I couldn't concentrate on why or what I would do there.

I kept thinking about the arrangement I had made with the woman I'd just met. I didn't even know her name.

If I had any sense, I thought, I'd leave her strictly alone. Let her play her mysterious games by herself.

But I knew I wouldn't.

Chapter 5

Virginia's flat was near Notting Hill, just off Bayswater Road, at the top of a modern block in one of the side streets running up to Church Street.

I climbed to the top landing and rang the bell. There was a tiny spyhole in the door and I heard a shuffling sound behind it. I could feel someone looking at me.

Suddenly the door opened and a woman was standing there.

'Come in,' she said. 'We've been waiting for you.'

This was about the last greeting I expected, and I wondered whether Tess Baker had rung her.

'Dick's in here,' she said, leading the way.

I followed her. She was wearing a pair of wide-legged jeans, cut narrow at the hips so that her buttocks rolled prettily as she walked. But her long brown hair hung straight and lank, and her face at the door had been haggard and feverish. She didn't look the type I'd expected, although her voice was Southern Counties, overlaid with the nasal London whine affected by women trying for street cred.

Dick was lying flat out on one of the leather sofas in the huge room. The curtains were drawn, but I could see that for a student flat the place was expensively furnished.

Dick raised himself on one arm and looked at me.

'How much have you got?' he said. His voice was so quiet I had to strain to hear it.

I spread my hands in a gesture of incomprehension.

'I came to see Virginia,' I said.

'Who the fuck are you?' Dick said, a bit louder this time.

'I'm looking for Virginia,' I said. 'Her parents asked me to give her a message.'

'Bloody hell,' Dick said, falling back into the sofa.

'She's not here,' the girl said. She moved back towards the door, her attitude suggesting that she was about to usher me out.

I stayed where I was.

'When did you see Virginia last?' I said.

The girl made a sound of disgust. She gave me a look of haughty indignation.

'I told Mrs Baker all that. Please go.'

'It was Mrs Baker who sent me,' I said. 'I'm just asking you about Virginia. It won't take long.'

'Shit,' said Dick from the sofa.

'There's nothing to tell,' the girl said. 'Now will you please go?'

'I told you that Mrs Baker sent me,' I said. I made a quick guess. 'When did you last pay your rent?'

'We don't pay rent,' the girl said.

'Okay. So you're here because you're friends of Virginia's, and if she doesn't come back, or her father decides he doesn't want you in her flat, you're right in the shit. And if that isn't enough, I can get the cops to come and have a look up here. See if you're holding anything.'

The girl looked uncertainly at the sofa, but Dick didn't move or make a sound.

They had to be addicts. Everything about them, their white, seamed faces, the drawn curtains, their lassitude, indicated heroin. Habitual users like this, at a desperate distance from shooting up, faced crisis with a pretence of normality which crumbled rapidly into hysteria or abject surrender.

'What do you want to know?' the girl asked.

'When did you see Virginia last?'

'I think it was – it's Wednesday today – it was two weeks ago exactly on a Wednesday. She came in with Roy and they went into her room for a while. Then they left.'

'What's Roy's last name?'

'I don't know. She never said.'

'How long has he been around?'

'After Christmas. I don't know. A few months.'

'Did she change a lot?'

'Yes. I suppose she did. She started being ratty all the time. Having a go at us.'

'How did you come to be sharing with her?'

'Dick used to be in the same class at college.'

'You're at college?' I asked Dick.

'He dropped out after the first year,' the girl said.

'Did she take anything with her?'

The girl sat down. She was getting tired from concentrating on my questions.

'What?'

'Did she take anything? Like clothes.'

'Yes. She took a toilet bag, and some of her clothes are missing.'

'Can I look at her room?'

'It's the second on the left.'

I went into the hallway and went through into a big room in the corner of the building.

The built-in wardrobe was open, with some dresses lying on the floor in front of it. A couple of the drawers at the bottom were open. Someone had used her makeup and left the table in a mess of sprinkled powder. A bottle was on its side leaking pink goo. A picture of her parents had been carefully torn in half and left lying by the bed.

The room looked deserted and ruined, ravaged by scavengers.

I went back into the living room. The couple hadn't moved.

'Did Virginia do smack?'

Neither of them answered, unless Dick's sigh counted as an answer.

'Did she do smack?' I shouted it this time at the top of my voice, loosing on them the anger I had begun to feel in Virginia's room.

'Yes,' the girl said sullenly.

'How long?'

'A couple of months.'

There was nothing more I wanted to ask. Smack was bad. I was prepared to hear that she was doing coke. Coke's self-image let its users down easy. It sold itself as a lighthearted goodtime drug. On coke you could get up and run. Even weak characters could get used to leaving it behind before their noses fell apart.

Heroin addicts smacked themselves in the head every day, and the longer they went on the worse it got. Even the threat of a quick death didn't discourage them.

I turned and walked out the hallway and down the stairs without saying anything more to the couple. Bullying them made me feel like I'd kicked a sick puppy.

Notting Hill had a bright new look, and for a moment I felt the tug of the shops, the urge to buy something. A record, a book, a new shirt – anything that would make me part of the transaction in which everyone else was engaged.

I hesitated in front of the tube station, looking around. But when I looked more closely, there was nothing that I wanted. There was nothing to do but go home.

So I went home.

Chapter 6

She was waiting for me in the lobby at five o'clock, and I asked her name before she could greet me.

'Sophie,' she said. 'What's yours?'

An hour later we were sitting in a pub tucked away in the maze of streets off Marylebone Road. It was one of those that had the renovated look of a wine bar, full of blond wood and lit by a circular globe, which threw off flashes of multi-coloured light.

We sat in a dark corner, hunched close to each other in order to hear over the noise of the jukebox.

'Did you know she was doing smack?' I asked.

Opposite me, Sophie's expression grew cautious. 'I suppose it's possible,' she said, 'living with Dick and Sally.'

'What do you mean?'

She shrugged.

'Well everyone knew Dick was a junkie. He couldn't concentrate half the time. You'd talk to him and he wouldn't hear you, you know?'

'How did he come to be sharing with Virginia then?'

'I think she liked him, and it was sort of fashionable then to be friendly with a real junkie. Everyone used to talk about helping them.'

She made a face, and it struck me that all I'd done so far was to ask her about Virginia. Perhaps it was time to change the subject.

'How do you come to be here?'

'You mean there?'

'That's right,' I said.

It was a question she seemed accustomed to answering. She came from Argentina, she said. Her father was a Scottish surveyor, who stayed long enough in Buenos Aires to marry her mother. She had worked for a newspaper, but the death squads had begun to pick up journalists and when the editor disappeared she decided it was time to go abroad.

'My mother was dead and I was afraid all the time.'

'Are you going back?'

She shrugged then shook her head.

'I don't know. Things haven't changed so much. Besides I am British. I have a British passport.'

'British people don't tell you they have a British passport.'

She stared at me seriously. Her eyebrows drew together. 'All right. I'm for Diego Maradona, and being here still makes me feel strange. I never knew my father. I went to the place where he came from. It meant nothing to me. I'm still trying to decide who I am and what to do.'

I nodded. I knew that feeling of not wanting to be where you were, but having nowhere else you wanted to be. The pleasures of exile.

'I enjoy being a photographer, but I don't make much. Teaching keeps me afloat.'

'It's hard all over,' I said.

She made a disgusted face at me. 'What do you do for a living? Apart from chasing Virginia around?'

I told her. She said she'd seen something I'd written. I felt the surprise I always felt. Most people don't notice the names.

I asked her about her work in Buenos Aires, and she began hesitantly, telling me about the city where she'd grown up. After a few sentences she gave me an odd look.

'My mother was black. A bit. Not so black as you, but you could see she had African blood.'

I nodded. I wasn't surprised. 'Is that a problem?'

She frowned. Then she shook her head slowly. 'No. Not here. In Argentina it was sometimes.'

Her eyes slid past mine and she gazed moodily at the bar. Somehow I knew that in a moment she would change the subject.

'How do you come to be looking for Virginia?' she asked. 'It's not just a message is it?'

'It's more than a message. Her parents are worried about her and they want me to locate her. See that she's okay.'

She looked puzzled. 'Why you?'

'I'm a sort of family friend.'

'You don't look much like the sort of friend that family has.'

'Keep an open mind,' I said.

She looked at me with raised eyebrows, then she smiled. 'I've been thinking since I saw you this morning. I've no idea where she is, but there was an address. About two months ago she asked me to a party, but it wasn't at her own flat. It sounded like one of those drug things. I didn't go, but I've got the address. She was off for a couple of days and somebody said she was staying there.'

She dug into her bag and took out a notebook. She gave me an address in W9 and I wrote it down.

'I'll be going now,' she said. 'I've got a lecture early.'

Although it was only ten o'clock, I didn't protest. There was a spark of attraction between us, but in recent times, I'd become cautious.

'How do I get in touch?'

She gave me a phone number. I leaned over and kissed her on the cheek, she smiled, and that was it. In a moment I was standing on the corner watching her walk rapidly towards the tube station.

I started to go home, but when I got there I changed my mind and got into the car. The address Sophie had given me wasn't far away and it was still early enough to take a look.

The street was in Paddington, down in the belt where it began to shade off into Harlesden, and halfway down the Harrow Road I turned off and parked near a shop where a little group of black teenagers were lounging around.

I got out the car and went past them, then, gripped by an unexpected reflex I turned back to stare. I'd suddenly been struck by the crazy idea that one of these boys might be Roy, but in the same moment I remembered that I didn't know what he looked like anyway.

I shook my head and walked on. I was jumping at shadows. But there was something spooky about the way my mind kept struggling to picture Roy, and somehow I kept seeing him as a younger version of myself.

The trouble was that everyone I'd spoken to had talked about Roy as a menacing and mysterious shadow. They knew nothing about him but his mere existence seemed to terrify them, and I knew something about that.

All those years ago, as a small boy in London, I had realised, with a shock I could still remember, that almost all the white people I came across were afraid of me.

I walked round the corner, and in a few steps made a detour to avoid a little knot of people gathered round an old lady who was sitting on a kitchen chair on the pavement.

As I approached they turned to glare at me, and I noticed that the old lady was bleeding from the nose. An old man stood next to her with his hand clutching her shoulder, and his eyes followed me with an expression in which fear and anger were nicely balanced. As I passed them I heard a voice, tremulous and outraged.

'Bleeding savages.'

Careful not to hurry I walked up the steps of the house I was looking for and rang the bell. Flat 3. As I did so I heard the wailing of a police siren. I looked towards the end of the road to see the cops arrive and missed the door opening.

'Can I help you?' someone said behind me.

An Indian girl was standing in the doorway. West Indian by her accent. Trinidad or Guyana. I couldn't be sure because living in England had rounded out and shortened her vowels.

'I'm looking for Virginia Baker,' I told her.

'Virginia Baker?' She looked amazed and slightly insulted. The impression was heightened by her appearance. She was short and had a large pouting chest, which gave her a strutting, indignant look.

'You probably want the fellow who was here before, mister,' she said.

Under the heavy black eyebrows her eyes flashed.

'You haven't been here long?'

'Only a couple of weeks.'

'Does the landlord live here?'

'Upstairs. On the top.'

She pointed the way, and watched me climb the stairs. All the

31

way up I could feel her eyes burning into the back of my neck.

When I knocked on the landlord's door there were some bumping noises and the sound of small feet scampering. I knocked again. Inside I heard a voice shouting something and the door opened suddenly. A short stocky black man with small red eyes and a bald head glared out at me. He stood half in and half out, one of his feet behind the door.

'Yes.'

'I was looking for the chap who used to live downstairs and the young lady there said you might know.'

'I might know? You mean flat 3?'

'Yes. Flat 3.'

'Who are you?'

He was from one of the small islands where a French patois was spoken, by the sound of him. They were usually friendly and polite people, but withdrawn and reserved according to Caribbean standards.

He wouldn't tell me any more than he had to, and besides he was one of the pugnacious kind, to judge by the way he looked at me.

'I'm a friend of his.'

'Tell him if you see him that I still want the rent.'

'Are we talking about the same man? What's his name?'

'Roy Baker. Half-caste.'

'Half-caste?' I was startled. No one had mentioned that.

He noticed my surprise.

'That's the same one?'

'Yes,' I said. 'The same one.'

He gave me a sneering grin. 'He owes you money too?'

'No.' I took a quick guess that he would have taken anything he found in the flat. 'He's got my stereo.'

He gave a quick glance backwards before he could stop himself, and then pulled the door almost shut behind him.

'I can't help you.'

'Okay. Thanks.'

I turned to go.

'Why don't you try his girlfriend? The white girl. You know her?'

I looked back. He was sneering at me again.

'Which one was that?'

He described someone who sounded like Virginia.

'She looked decent at first, but she had nasty habits.'

'What?'

He came closer. Disapproval crossed his face followed by a lubricious glee.

'I saw her coming out of there sometimes. Everything hanging outside. Staggering. She could barely walk. You know what I mean? She used to give me a look, but I wouldn't touch no junkie girl. Dirty.'

'You must have been up all night to catch your look, eh.'

He stiffened and I turned away, then he said something in patois which sounded nasty and slammed the door.

Outside in the street I took a deep breath after the cramped, airless atmosphere of the house. The old lady, the old man and the police had all gone. It was nearly twelve, the pubs were closed and the streets were empty, except for the odd group of youths standing in front of a kebab shop or clustered on the corner.

As I came up to the car a pair of tall black youths passed me, and I gave them a little wave of the hand. One of them nodded back suspiciously. As I unlocked the door I chuckled to myself, remembering the time when I'd been walking along with my son, and I'd spoken to a black driver lounging against the side of his coach. It was about the Test score, I think, and when we'd gone past my son asked me if I knew the man. I told him no.

'Why did you speak to him?'

In the old days, I explained, when I'd first come to Britain, black people used to speak to each other when we met in the street. We'd ask about the news from home or the cricket or what it was like in a strange district or where to find lodgings, or we'd speak just because it was sort of reassuring to be in contact with another black person. If anything happened you would look for another black person to help you.

'What would happen?'

'You might be attacked. That used to happen.'

'That doesn't happen much any more,' he said. 'Talking to each other I mean.'

'Some people do it,' I said. 'I do it.'

'Yes.' He was silent for a moment. 'People still get attacked though, Dad. Not us. But it's happening to Asians all the time.'

33

Remembering the conversation it struck me that in another ten years or so my son would be leaving his teens, growing up, adult. I wondered for a moment what sort of friends he would have, and I hoped that he wouldn't be confused and fugitive like the youth I was chasing. I wondered too whether Roy's father knew where he was.

I was too worked up and depressed to go home. So I drove up to Alexandra Palace and sat in the car looking out over the silent grounds to the lights of North London beyond. Behind me crouched the massive pile of old bricks and broken glass. It started out being built as the North Londoners' own Royal residence and was never finished.

Whenever I saw it something in me vibrated at the thought of all that craft and material wasted. Arson and vandalism had stolen any nobility it once had, and now it was merely a scruffy ruin. Yet it was one of my favourite places in London, and on that evening it matched my mood.

I was no closer to Virginia, but I was becoming more and more interested in Roy Baker. It was an odd coincidence that they had the same name. Perhaps he only used the name, indulging in some wayward fantasy of borrowing her identity. Perhaps the name was real and had been the basis of a tie that bound them together.

Whichever it was, it was beginning to sound as if the Bakers ought to find their daughter quick. Whatever trouble she was in, Roy would be in it too. But the difference between them meant that where she could float, he would struggle and sink.

I was tired and when I thought of Roy Baker I seemed to see my son's face. It gave me a pain like a hand gripping my heart, and I started the engine in a hurry and drove home.

Chapter 7

When I rang the Bakers in the morning Tess answered.

'Hello,' she said.

'Samson Dean.'

'Mr Dean. I was just about to ring you.'

'Good,' I said. 'I was hoping to speak to you and Mr Baker.'

'Ah. My husband's away at the moment, but you can speak to me. Would you like to come here? About eleven.'

'Yes.'

She put the phone down. The conversation had been brief and her tone curt. I wondered whether they were already regretting the deal. I doubted that what I had to tell them would make things any better.

As it turned out, what Tess had to tell me was more important.

She took me into the kitchen and gave me a cup of coffee from the pot that was standing on the table.

'We've had good news,' she said.

She smiled, but something about the way she sat forward in her seat and gripped her cup made that seem unlikely.

'We've heard from Virginia,' she said. 'She's staying with a girlfriend, someone she used to be at school with. She just took off on the spur of the moment, and it only occurred to her to ring this morning. She's usually very responsible, but I suppose we keep forgetting that she's only a child.'

'How did she sound?'

'Oh, well enough. She's fine. So there's no need for you to bother any more. In fact I'm sorry we wasted your time, but actually we're very grateful to you for your help, even though there was nothing wrong. My husband asked me to tell you how grateful we both were.'

'Oh. I thought you said he was away.'

She flashed me a cold look that told me I was being impertinent. 'He rang me. In any case I don't think we should take up any more of your time.'

She stared at me with an angry condescension, but the droop of her shoulders and the way she twisted her fingers together contradicted her expression.

'Yes,' I said, 'but perhaps I should tell you what happened.'

She nodded and sat back. I told her about Virginia's flatmates, about Roy Baker and her daughter's visits to the flat in Paddington. As I talked she fidgeted, shifted in her seat and looked at her watch. Before I had finished she interrupted me abruptly.

'This really is very useful,' she said, 'but I have an appointment in a short while. I'm sorry.'

I got up and she saw me to the door.

'Thank you again,' she said, and shut the door firmly in my face.

The gesture rankled as I drove back. Worse. Somehow I hadn't believed a word she'd said, but I had the feeling that she didn't care what I thought.

She hadn't mentioned the money she'd given me but we both knew that I wouldn't have had time to spend it looking for her daughter. If I didn't send it back it would look as if I'd simply pocketed it.

In effect that was precisely what I had done, but now it made me feel like a thief or a blackmailer.

When we first met they'd treated me as an equal, but now, I thought angrily, it was obvious that they saw me as someone who they could call in to do a dirty job, then dismiss. It struck me also that there had been fear and contempt not far below the surface when they talked about Roy.

I was black too, and the way Tess had slammed the door in my face was probably just what she'd have liked to do to him.

She must have predicted greed and dishonesty on my part, I

thought, and she would say that it was money well spent just to get rid of me. The idea made me literally squirm with rage, and I slammed my fist against the dashboard. The car swerved a little, and the van behind gave me a long blast of the horn.

I put both hands back on the wheel, but I didn't feel any better. The phrase the bank manager had used in his letter came back to my mind. I'd never believed myself dishonoured by his stopping my cheques, but the way Tess had behaved gave me exactly that feeling.

I knew that if I left the situation as it was I'd feel shame and anger whenever I thought about the Bakers. I couldn't do anything about the money, so my only course was to continue. They'd told me to stop but it was my choice what I did. At least if I poked around enough to justify the expenditure I could escape from the situation with some dignity. I had the sense also, that if I exposed the lie Tess had told me it would be a kind of revenge.

Perhaps, I thought, I was just being stubborn. Chip on my shoulder.

'So what?' I said out loud. 'Nobody tells me what to do.'

I would continue looking for Roy and Virginia, I decided, until I thought it was time to stop, and to hell with what the Bakers said.

I ran through the conversation with Tess again. The call from Virginia that morning seemed too much of a coincidence, and in any case everything I'd found out seemed to point to a drama playing itself out. Virginia's sudden appearance in rural England was too good to be true.

I stopped at some phone booths outside Battersea Park. Two were vandalised, but the other one still worked. I rang Pete, and got the Commons answering service. I tried again and got Baker's secretary. She said Pete and the boss had gone up to the constituency. They had left early in the morning to drive up there and they wouldn't be back till the next day.

Driving through Chelsea I thought it over. This wasn't proof but it seemed strange that Baker should ring home halfway through a trip up the motorway. On the other hand, even if he hadn't, it didn't prove that Tess was lying.

There was nothing I could do about it. But I was still involved. That moment in the car near Ally Pally seemed to have welded me to the fate of the missing couple. Now I felt aimless and dull, as if I'd lost my grip on something important.

As if it knew what I felt the car hovered uncertainly, and when we got to Marble Arch I let it go down Bayswater Road to Notting Hill.

There was no answer when I rang on the bell at Virginia's flat. I wondered where they were. They couldn't have gone far. Addicts like Dick and Sally couldn't afford to stray far from home.

I went round the corner to buy a paper, then came back and sat in the car reading it. I had just worked my way through an article on Sri Lanka when I saw them coming. I got out of the car and walked in front of them as they were about to enter the block. Dick looked at me dully and tried to walk round me. I got in his way again.

'Hi Dick,' I said. 'Remember me?'

I couldn't tell whether or not he did until he spoke.

'Fuck off,' he said. He sounded a little more vigorous this morning.

'Come on, Dick,' I said. 'Don't be like that. I've come to do you a favour. Have you heard from Virginia?'

Dick looked at his girlfriend. I couldn't work out what that meant.

'Her mother's heard from her,' I said. 'She's in the country with an old schoolfriend.'

'Do you hear that, Sally?' Dick said. 'She's in the country with an old schoolfriend.'

He sounded sarcastic in a laid-back way. Sally laughed, a sort of muffled shriek, but when the sound stopped there was nothing amused about her face.

'What's funny about that?' I asked. 'Do you know where she is?'

'Piss off,' Dick said.

They walked round me again and went in. I thought about going after them but I wasn't sure what the point would be. I was sure though, that they weren't impressed by my news.

It was little enough, but when I put their manner together with Tess Baker's edginess, my suspicions were confirmed.

I rang Sophie and after she told me she was fine and I told her I was fine, we arranged to meet later on. I wasn't sure that it was a good idea, but I didn't have any work on hand, and besides, I couldn't get her out of my mind. I kept thinking about her mother who was a bit black, and wondering what she felt about that.

It was a curious circle. Brooding about Roy and Sophie brought me back to my son, and focused my worries and fears about him. I looked at my watch. It was gone three o'clock and he would be out of school soon, so I drove up to Camden Town.

Outside the school gates a small knot of women was waiting. They stared at me curiously, and one of them, who recognised me, smiled quickly, then turned away.

In a moment we heard the raised, shrieking voices of the children as they poured out of the doors. My son came streaking out of the gates ahead of the others, and he was past me before he realised I was there. He drew up and turned back to hug me.

'Hello Dad. What are you doing here?'

'Wanted to see you.'

We walked along. I took him to a corner shop to buy sweets, but all he wanted was some bubble gum and a computer magazine. The walk didn't take long and after our first greeting there didn't seem much to say. I asked him about school, and how things were at home, about his bicycle. His answer to everything was 'all right'.

When he got to the door I lingered on the pavement watching, while he turned the key and went in. As he disappeared he gave me a last wave.

Going back I felt worse than I had before. Kids. Your parents fuck you up, I thought, but deep inside me I felt the tug of identity with the parents of kids like Roy and Virginia or the parents of any kids in trouble.

By the time I went to meet Sophie I had decided what I would do, and I'd also decided to try and put the Bakers and their problems out of my mind for a bit.

It wasn't easy.

We went to a restaurant just off Edgware Road. On the way we'd agreed not to talk about Virginia, but the subject kept cropping up.

'I was thinking about Virginia Baker,' she said suddenly.

39

'Having a famous father may not be a big deal at Oxford or Cambridge, but it does sort of mark her out here, and she's got a runny attitude. I only heard her talk about him once or twice, but it was always kind of disparaging, as if she really disliked him.'

'Maybe she felt stifled,' I said.

'Well it sounded like more than that. Really bitter. The English have peculiar relations with their parents, and half the girls talk resentfully about their lives at home, but with her it's extreme.'

'Like hatred?'

'Yes. No. It's hard to tell isn't it? Love and hate. It's all passion. Probably works the same in the end.'

'What about your mother?' I said. 'Did you get on with her?'

She frowned, and for a moment she stared at me as if deciding whether or not to answer.

'Yes.' She shook her head irritably. 'In a way. She was a wonderful woman.'

She stopped.

'Some time,' she said, 'when I know you better I'll tell you about her.'

Parents and children. She looked away from me, and I found myself wondering what my son would say about me when someone asked the inevitable question.

Afterwards we walked slowly up to my flat. It was past closing time, but the streets were still busy. On the corners knots of young Arabs stood in clusters, chattering and staring at Sophie as we went past. By now most of the women walking around were prostitutes. The Arabs hissed and called out as they went by, and a few times we passed one of the women arguing out a bargain with a little group of men.

This was a tradition of the area.

A hundred yards away had been the site of public gallows near Marble Arch where carnival crowds had watched men and women die, and the whole district had been one of the most disreputable and dangerous places in the growing capital.

'It still gives me the creeps,' Sophie said, 'even if it is history.'

Her tone had something angry about it, and when I glanced round I could see that her face was set in tight cold lines.

'All of you in this country,' she said, 'talk about violence and terror and poverty as if it was a story in a book. Believe me, there are places where such things happen all the time.'

I could have argued about that, but I didn't reply because it occurred to me immediately that she might be thinking about her own experience. At the same time, for no reason, the picture of their daughter that the Bakers had shown me flashed into my mind.

If I was right and she hadn't come back, then something terrible might have happened.

As if she sensed my change in mood, Sophie linked her arm through mine and leaned on me a little. When I looked round she was smiling.

'Where are we going?' she asked me. In the reflected light of the street lamps her eyes were glowing.

'I'll give you three guesses,' I said.

Chapter 8

I didn't get up until about noon. It was a Saturday, and somehow the spring that got me moving most days had wound down.

The problem was that I'd decided, during the night, to spend the day hanging around Notting Hill waiting to see whether Virginia or Roy would come back.

I wasn't looking forward to the prospect, but by the early afternoon I managed to pull myself together and leave the flat.

I took along a couple of books I had meant to read for a while. Unless someone turned up right away it would be a long wait.

I parked up the road from Virginia's flat, just in sight of the windows, and after a couple of hours reading the newspapers I slumped back in my seat and daydreamed.

As always, being in Notting Hill took me back to those years in the fifties when I'd been at school and London was still a mysterious, exciting and dangerous place.

I had been on the bus coming home from school one evening, when I read about the Notting Hill riots in a fellow passenger's paper. It was a shock I still remembered, shrinking in my window seat, my body already cringing with the pain of being hit by iron bars, as the paper had described.

As I stood on the platform the conductress, a yellow-haired lady with a kind face, looked down at me and smiled.

'Run home and be careful,' she said.

'If I ever get home,' I said angrily.

I was only ten, but I knew enough to be angry. Her face fell. 'We're not all like that,' she said.

Sitting in my car at Notting Hill, the memory of that time was strange and dreamlike, as if it had happened in another country to someone else.

I must have fallen asleep then, because when I woke up, my head was aching and my eyes burning, it was dark and the lights were on in Virginia's flat. If anything had happened I would have missed it, and I wondered what to do.

In the end I decided to stay where I was. It was only about eight, and I comforted myself with the reflection that if either of the two turned up, it was likely to be late.

A few hours passed, and a number of people went in and out of the block of flats but I spotted no one likely. Two or three people looked as if they might be visitors for Dick, but by midnight they had left.

I was thinking about leaving myself as one o'clock approached. The street was now deserted except for the occasional drunk, or the odd little group of young people in party clothes.

Suddenly a black custom-built car came round the corner and stopped in front of the flat. The front grille glowed with red spotlights and a string of amber lights winked on and off in the back window. As the car went past I had heard the beat of reggae music.

The driver got out, locked the door carefully and swaggered into the doorway of the building. He was a bearded black man wearing a fawn three-piece suit with matching shoes, topped off by a brown and white woollen hat with a bobble on it.

I sat up. This looked an interesting prospect. He wasn't mixed race so he couldn't be Roy, but he could be connected in some way.

I got out of the car and stood closer to the doorway, but after fifteen minutes I went back. It was another hour before he came out, and then he was carrying a stereo.

He put it in the boot of his car and went back up. A few minutes later he came out again with a TV set. He made two more trips with a video machine and then a large suitcase, which he carried as if it was heavy.

It seemed that the couple was selling off the contents of the flat, and I wondered whether they'd decided to do a runner.

43

I crossed the road and came up behind the man just as he was closing the boot.

'Hey bro,' I said.

I wasn't sure how I was going to carry on the conversation but that was as far as I got.

He turned faster than I could move, and hit me in the stomach. I saw the blow coming but I was falling to the pavement, gasping for breath and clutching at my midriff before I could react.

He walked unhurriedly away, and I heard the car door slam. Before I could get up he was driving away, the amber window lights blinking as if in mockery.

I got up, leaning on the wall, breathing deeply. There was no one around to see the incident, and for a moment I asked myself if it had really happened. I went back to the car and sat down, rubbing the spot.

The windows of the flat were still lit, and it struck me that the man's reaction must have meant that he had stolen the stuff, either from Virginia's flat or somewhere else.

I got out again and climbed the stairs, my legs feeling weak and rubbery. I rang on the bell. No answer. I rang again, then I noticed that the door moved a little when I pressed on the bell. It was still locked but when I pushed a thin crack appeared between the door and the frame. I pushed and listened. No sound, although the lights were on.

I rang again then pushed hard with my shoulder. All of a sudden the door sprang open with a bang.

I went in.

A light was on in the hallway and in the room beyond.

'Dick. Sally,' I called out.

No answer. I called out again and walked slowly into the room.

The couple were lying on the sofa. Dick was stretched out in a comfortable pose, while Sally lay with her head on his lap.

I called out their names again. They didn't move and I leaned forward and shook Dick, who collapsed sideways, his hand trailing over the side of the sofa on to the floor. I felt his pulse, then Sally's. I couldn't feel anything.

They had looked peaceful and relaxed but now I could see they were dead.

I backed away slowly and went for the door. Then I stopped and forced myself to go into Virginia's room. It was even more of a mess, with drawers sprawling open, and clothes strewn around. The wardrobe had been partly cleared out, and I was certain that some bottles and jars had gone from the makeup table.

I went back to the sitting room and looked around, averting my eyes from Dick and Sally. I couldn't work out whether anything besides the TV and stereo was gone, so I left, moving as quickly as I could.

Downstairs, I peeped round the doorway to make sure that no one was in the street to see me, then ran for the car and drove away.

Near Marble Arch I stopped at the row of phone booths. There were six of them, but only one worked. In the others the phones were neatly ripped out and laid on the floor. As I opened the only intact booth the smell of urine hit me. The walls were scrawled with numbers and names.

'PUNISHMENT FOR BEGINNERS ' 'EBONY ' 'FRENCH
MAID ' 'RUBBER GIRL '

I dialled 999 and when they answered I said that there'd been an accident. I gave them the address and told them that there were two dead people there. Then I hung up, ignoring their requests for my name and address.

I drove home in a state of shock. When I turned off Edgware Road and stopped, my hands were trembling where they gripped the wheel. I had seen death before, but the sickening blow, the silent flat, the smooth stiff faces of the couple, all haunted me.

It looked like an overdose, but it was hard to believe in an overdose happening accidentally to both of them at the same time. The presence of the man in the woollen hat and the rifling of the flat also worried me. He had taken away some of Virginia's things, which might indicate that she was somehow involved. I didn't know how, and anyway, it might be mere coincidence.

I went to bed, and had a nightmare in which someone was standing over me, watching me. I got up and made myself a cup of tea. It was already light and I sat by the window looking out.

There was no point, I thought, in going to tell the Bakers about the deaths, because I wasn't certain of their importance.

In the distance I heard the sound of drums and bagpipes. Round the corner came a little procession led by a band of girls dressed in kilts. Behind them walked a little group of priests and an altar boy, followed by a group of marching people. Opposite my window the pipes stopped and they marched on, eerily, to the sombre banging of the single drum.

Gooseflesh crept up the back of my neck. The mournful pacing of the priests, the sight of uniforms, brought me more echoes of death.

This was an area in which a number of bombs had gone off. In the next street a couple of Arabs had blown themselves into chunks of meat, and every fortnight or so there would be a bomb scare, with white tape across the road and the flashing blue lights of ambulances.

The procession could have been quaint and colourful, but to me it looked merely menacing.

Turning away from the window I ran over my alternatives. I couldn't get any more out of Virginia's flat. The Bakers were unlikely to help me, and even if Virginia had come back home, I probably wouldn't get to see her. That left Roy's old address.

The drums were receding, but the sound was still getting on my nerves and I banged the window shut. Suddenly there was silence in the room.

'Wish it was as easy as that,' I muttered to the kitchen stove.

Chapter 9

I drove down to Paddington in a mood of resignation. This would be my last attempt. If nothing happened I would have to give up.

There was no answer when I rang the landlord's bell. For a moment I hovered uncertainly, but then I remembered it was Sunday and the family would be at church. I went back to the car and sat in it.

After about half an hour I saw him. He was walking at the head of the little family, his wife in a discreetly flowered hat, a white dress and white shoes, two teenagers, a boy and a girl, followed by three other children, the youngest about five. I waited till they'd gone in and then went over, climbed the stairs and rang the bell. He opened the door right away.

'What do you want?' he said. 'You found him?'

'No,' I said. 'I'm still trying. Have you got any of the things from his room? I want to look at them. Maybe I can find an address or something.'

'I've looked already,' he said. 'There's nothing.'

'Can I look?' I said. 'If I find him I'll tell you right away.'

'I don't have anything really,' he said.

'I don't want to take anything,' I said. 'I just want to take a look. Books, records, anything like that.'

'Anything I got from that room is legally mine,' he said sharply.

'Sure,' I said. 'Of course. I just want a look.'

He stared at me for a moment, then he stood back.

'Come in.'

I walked into the hallway.

'Just stand there,' he said.

I stood.

He opened a cupboard near the front door, and took out a couple of boxes. One of them contained a few books, mostly thrillers and soft porn, a bedside lamp, a bottle of aftershave and a couple of old magazines, *Tatler* and *Cosmopolitan*. Odd.

I turned to the other box which contained some records and clothes, bundled up shirts and a couple of pairs of trousers. He might have taken most of his property with him, but I had the feeling that there wasn't much more in the first place.

I grimaced.

Take away my telly and my video, and except for some books and shirts, there wouldn't be much more to show for my life.

'You come from Manchester too?' the landlord said.

'I've lived there,' I said.

'You don't have an accent like him,' he told me, 'half the time I could hardly understand him.'

I riffled through the records. One of them had a label stuck to the jacket. Printed on it was the name of a record shop in Withington Road, Manchester.

'He could have gone back to Manchester,' I said.

'It could be,' the landlord said, 'but he told me that he was never going back. That kind of boy, he was probably running from something. Probably he couldn't go back.'

His tone was speculative. But if he hoped I would tell him some juicy details he was out of luck.

I picked up a record by U-Roy. Classical dub. Ten years ago when I was in Manchester, dub was all the rage.

I pulled it out of the jacket and looked at the label. Scrawled in the middle was a name. Roy Akimbola. I put it back and stood up.

'Thank you,' I told the landlord.

'You see?' he said. 'Nothing at all.'

I nodded. 'Sorry to waste your time.'

I went down the stairs smiling. At least I had a name and a place where Roy had come from. I knew more about him now than I had before.

Chapter 10

I drove home through the quiet Sunday streets. In Edgware Road crowds of Arabs were already walking up and down, and sitting in front of the restaurants at pavement tables.

In the flat I looked up Pete's telephone number and rang him. When he answered he sounded curiously formal and distant in comparison with his manner when he answered the office phone.

'Pete, I want to see you today.'

'I'd love to see you, Samson, but today's a bit difficult. I haven't been home for ages, and I have to spend some time with my family.'

A wife and two kids, perfect for a political aspirant.

'Sorry Pete, but a number of things have happened which concern people we both know. I have to speak to you and I don't want to do it on the phone.'

'Okay,' he said. 'Meet me by the pond on the Common, round about five.'

That was Clapham Common, not very far away from where the Bakers lived. I lay back in my single armchair and began going through the papers. There were no references to Baker.

Later on I drove down to Clapham over Chelsea Bridge. I was early, and I stood by the pond watching the model boats which were being sailed by a few men accompanied by small boys. They were all radio controlled, and they moved around the pond with a high buzzing sound. A short distance away some young men were kicking a ball around. In other parts of the Common couples strolled or lay on the grass.

I saw Pete coming from a distance as he rounded the corner of the church. He was holding a leash and a hairy sort of terrier bounded along behind him. Another surprise. Pete had always disliked dogs. He must have changed.

He was wearing designer casuals. A light blue zipped-up jacket, white linen trousers and white shoes. I was wearing white shoes, cream-coloured trousers and a white silk shirt.

As Pete came up he grinned at me.

'Nice shoes,' he said. 'So crime does pay.'

'You ought to know,' I said. 'The white-collar variety pays best.'

He laughed, then frowned and shouted at the dog as it ran towards the pond. 'Jason,' he called out.

'Jason?' I said. 'Oh shit. That's unbelievable.'

'He's my wife's,' he said. 'I can't stand the bugger.'

I'd read somewhere that Pete had married a minor heiress and it hadn't surprised me. He'd had a posh front at college, but at the time he couldn't afford a car or any of the other things the rich students had. Times had obviously changed.

'What's going on, Pete?'

'I don't know,' he said. 'You tell me.'

'I'm talking about Virginia. Is she really in the country?'

'I suppose she is,' he said. 'Why do you doubt it?'

'How do you know about it?'

'Tess told me.'

'Just like she told me,' I said. 'I didn't believe her. When she told me she was twitching like a crazy woman. There was something wrong.'

'That might be nothing to do with it.'

He looked irritable and he shouted for the dog again.

'In any case,' he said, 'I really shouldn't be discussing all this behind Baker's back. It's nothing to do with me.'

'You're full of shit, Pete,' I said. 'Don't forget you brought me into this. The problem is that I want to know a little more about Virginia and her relations with her parents. That sort of stuff. Indulge me. Christ, no one's actually told me anything.'

'It doesn't matter now,' he said. 'She's back. You can forget about it.'

50

'Even if it was true,' I replied, 'that's not all there is to it.'

I told him what I'd found out about Virginia's habits, and her involvement with drugs. Then I told him about Dick and Sally. When I told him how I'd found them dead he stopped strolling and stared at me.

'My God,' he muttered.

'Right now,' I said, 'the cops are probably knocking on Baker's door to find out, very politely of course, if he knows that two junkies are dead in his daughter's flat. It won't cause him any real problems. After all Virginia's been away on holiday for a couple of weeks. She's not to know what's going on. I don't suppose they'll even want her for the inquest. Open and shut. Two junkies taking an overdose. It's a little unusual but it happens often enough.'

'You're right,' he said slowly. 'There's no evidence that Virginia had anything to do with any of it.'

'No. But the guy who punched me outside the flat took away some of her personal belongings. Dresses. Makeup. That kind of thing. Why?'

Pete shrugged. He stood still, turned away from me, staring after the dog.

'Let's suppose for a moment,' I said, 'that they're covering up something. There are a number of alternatives. She could be mixed up in some kind of crime. She could have been kidnapped. Whatever.'

'Melodrama,' Pete said.

'What happened yesterday was pretty melodramatic,' I said. He spread his hands in a puzzled gesture.

'What am I supposed to do?'

'Help me,' I said. 'Just a little. Tell me more about them.'

'What good will that do?'

'I don't know.'

Pete looked pale and tense. He slammed at the ground with his heel.

'Tell me about Virginia,' I said. 'Has she been peculiar lately?'

'Yes. Well she's been behaving a little oddly recently. Till a couple of months ago she seemed a serious type. In comparison with some of her schoolfriends. She wanted to be a photographer and it wasn't just an idle whim. A few months ago she started going a bit mad. She stopped coming home and when she did, or when they went to see her, there were a lot of rows. They shouted at each other.'

'That's not totally abnormal for adolescents, is it?'

'Well no. But she'd never been difficult. Give her what she wanted and she was quite happy. Polite. Well mannered.'

'What about boyfriends?'

'No one steady, you know.'

'What about this black boy? You know he's named Baker? Roy Baker.'

'I hadn't heard his name.'

He paused, frowning.

'There was something with two black men last year. I didn't get all the details. I was on holiday so I was away for most of it. But it seemed that a black man came to Baker's house and insisted on seeing him. He was trying to blackmail Baker in some way. He had a photograph of someone he said was Baker and a black lady.'

'Baker?'

'Oh no. It was a very old photo apparently, and it was impossible to tell who it was. He said it was a picture of Baker as a student, but of course it wasn't. Baker called the police.'

'And no one ever got hold of the story?'

'He didn't press charges. He didn't have to. When the police went to question the guy, he and another man attacked them. They went away for a year. Assault. That was the end of it.'

'Was it a naughty picture?'

'Not according to Baker. Anyway it seemed unlikely. They were just trying it on. You'd be surprised at the sort of crap MPs have to put up with, begging letters, threats, cranks, nuts. You should see the stuff I look at every day. Most of it is unconvincing or inefficient or crazy.'

'Do you know these guys' names?'

'No.'

'Can you find out?'

'Sure.'

'Where was Baker at university?'

'Cambridge. Then he did business at Manchester. The gritty North. Getting close to the people.'

'Is that what it says in *Who's Who*?'

'No. You read that between the lines.'

We stood in silence watching the dog chase around. The sun was now low on the horizon and it was chilly. I shivered.

'I must be getting back,' Pete said. 'That dog's had more exercise than it can stand.'

'I'll ring you,' I said.

He nodded and walked away.

I drove back slowly, thinking hard. Everything I found out seemed to link all the Bakers to some sort of craziness. I was sure that they wouldn't help by telling me whatever it was they were trying to conceal. I would have to unravel the ball of string from the other end.

Perhaps it would be easier if I obeyed my instincts and followed the signs that pointed to Roy's trail.

I rang my son. His mother answered. She said he was upset because his new BMX bike had been stolen. Apparently she had dropped him off with a friend at a cycle track in Shepherd's Bush, and a couple of big gypsy boys had come along and ripped off the bikes.

'I didn't think,' she said.

I choked down my anger and panic. He could have been hurt.

'Can I talk to him?'

When he came on the line his voice was subdued.

'Hello Dad.'

'I hear you had some trouble.'

He told me the story all over again. There had been no grown ups supervising.

'You mean you just stood there and let them take all your stuff?'

He was silent.

'You must always fight,' I said. 'If your bike was important you should have fought them. Then they might have run away.'

He said nothing. I could hear him breathing.

'I'm sorry, son,' I said quickly. 'You didn't do anything wrong.'

'You should have seen them, Dad. They're big and dirty. Those gypsy kids are bad. They like fighting and hurting people.'

'Okay,' I said. 'I understand.'

'They call us names.'

'What sort of names?'

'You know. Like people shout out of cars. Nigger, half-caste.'

'Well we talked about that before. Usually that's because they're afraid of you. It's to do with them, not to do with you.'

'I hate those gypsies,' he said suddenly.

'You're angry with them, and that's all right. But hate is different. They're probably miserable to do what they did. You don't have to hate them.'

'I still hate them,' he said. 'You don't know what they're like, Dad. They're vicious.'

'Maybe they are,' I said, 'But that's not what you have to learn. You have to learn that things and places have meanings like words and you can read them as you would a book. Think of a car coming fast down the road, and you're standing behind a parked van. That's like a sentence that has a meaning.'

'Right,' he said. 'I've got it. If there's a gypsy camp near the cycle track, and there are no adults around, that means a stolen bike.'

From the tone of his voice, he was teasing me.

'I may be going to Manchester for a couple of days,' I said. Until that moment I hadn't decided.

'Why?'

'I'm just going to do a little job,' I said.

'Okay,' he said. 'I'll see you when you get back?'

'Yes.'

He said goodbye and put the phone down. I felt terrible, agitated and melancholy at the same time. When I arrived in London as a child I had learned to read the city like the strange map it was, scanning it carefully for danger and interest, studying how the people and places were organised. Everything meant something.

I wanted to pass that on to my son, but I kept getting the feeling that his maps had different meanings.

Chapter 11

I woke up late with a feeling of frustration. I had dreamed about a political meeting, where I'd been standing by the platform waiting to deliver an important speech about being black in Britain.

But though I put my hand up and waved and argued with the people sitting near me, I wasn't called.

When I woke up I realised that there was a political party conference on TV. I switched it off and rang Pete at his office.

'Did you find out the names?' I asked him.

'Yes. Akimbola and Ford. No fixed abode I think. But they came from Manchester.'

I put the phone down and rang George, a friend who lived in Manchester. No answer.

I pondered for a moment. Then I made the decision. I had to go in a hurry, before I changed my mind.

I put a few clothes in a bag, ran down the stairs, and took a bus down to Euston, my favourite railway station. Unlike Paddington, or Waterloo, it was all new and shiny, with no echoes of tradition or decay.

I had meant to buy a book, but I had to run for the train, and there wasn't enough time. Instead I looked out of the window, and after a while I fell asleep.

The train got in close to four o'clock. I thought about taking a taxi but at this hour of the day there was a long queue, and I decided to walk. Besides, I wasn't sure where I was going. I strolled down to Piccadilly, then turned left and down to St Peter's Square. From there I walked through to Oxford Road.

I knew where I was going now. My feet had taken me to the local radio station where I used to work. I'd be able to use the phone there.

The blonde at the reception was a woman I remembered from ten years earlier. She recognised me and smiled.

'Go on in,' she said.

I went on in. The newsroom where I'd once worked looked the same, a familiar mixture of efficiency and untidiness.

John, a short Welshman with a pugnacious air, and a plaque which said 'news editor' in front of him, got up from his desk and shook my hand.

'What are you doing here?'

I shrugged.

'Just visiting.'

He'd read some of my articles, he told me, in the national newspapers. I was in the big time. I looked at his expression to see whether he was kidding me, but he wasn't. Going to London and making a living was success. Some of my former colleagues had spent half their working lives dreaming about moving on, down to London.

I told him I wanted to use the phone. He nodded.

'Sorry,' he said. 'I've got to go. News bulletin.'

He went. I sat down at the table and rang George.

No answer.

I picked up the phone book and checked the name Akimbola without much hope, but there were three, two in Longsight, and one in Moss Side. I dialled the one in Moss Side. It had been disconnected. I rang the other two and asked for Roy. There was no such person at either number.

I went out and got a taxi to Moss Lane. I remembered the Harp Lager building, but the rest of the landscape had changed so much as to be unrecognisable.

It gave me a curious feeling of unease, as if they'd done all this while my back was turned, deliberately obscuring all the familiar signs so that I no longer understood the idiom of the city.

The taxi drew up at a row of houses which hadn't been there ten years before, opposite the sprawling Hulme estate. A few hundred yards away was the original site of Henry Royce's first workshop. It had been a different city then.

I knocked at the address I'd got out of the phone book. There was a shuffling sound and a black lady in her forties and dressed in white overalls came to the door. She looked at me suspiciously, without speaking.

'I'm looking for Roy Akimbola,' I said.

'He doesn't live here any more,' she said.

She started to close the door but I put my hand against it.

'Could I speak to you? Are you his mother?'

'Who are you?' she said. 'What do you want?'

She was nearly as tall as I was, and I could see that she was once a good-looking woman. She had the characteristic look of mixed-race women in Liverpool and Manchester. During adolescence and their early twenties they could be spectacular, at once delicate and fierce, exotic and athletic.

This lady's hair was speckled with grey and her eyes glared with the shadow of pain.

'I'm Samson Dean,' I said. 'I used to live round there in Withington Road,' I pointed. 'I just wanted to talk to Roy.'

'Well he's not here,' she said, 'and I'm his auntie, not his mother. I haven't seen him for over a year now.'

'He might be in trouble,' I said. 'I'm trying to help him.'

'He's always in trouble. I don't want to know. Did he send you?'

'No.' I took a deep breath. 'I want to ask you some things that might help him.'

'I don't know anything about him,' she said irritably.

'He's mixed up in some funny business,' I said. 'It might have something to do with what happened here years ago.'

She looked puzzled, but she said nothing. Behind us a voice called out. Along the path came a young white woman pushing a pram. A little mixed-race boy trotted along by her elbow. We both cooed at him and the girl went past us smiling, then turned into a house two doors up.

As we turned back to face each other our eyes met, and for the first time she smiled at me.

She stepped back from the door. 'Come in,' she said.

I sat and waited while she made a cup of tea. Her name was Shirley, she told me. Her sister had died ten years ago and she'd brought up Roy since then. He was a difficult boy though, who'd been sent away for the first time when he was fourteen.

The mantelpiece was lined with photographs of Roy at various stages of his development, and with pictures of the two sisters.

The tea was sweet and milky. Shirley sat opposite me comfortably. Now she had decided to talk to me she was friendly and warm.

'Why's he calling himself Baker?' I asked her.

She looked startled. 'I don't know,' she said. 'But that's his father's name.'

'What?'

'My sister Grace always told him his father was dead, but he never believed it. You know what it's like round here. They know everything that goes on.'

'Somebody told him.'

'They must have done. Everyone round here knew about it. But that were twenty year ago, and most of them have moved or died.'

She sighed, got up and fiddled with one of the pictures. It showed two small girls with a black man in Air Force uniform.

'Of course he always denied it. But I knew. He was the father.'

I watched her in silence.

'He was posh,' she said. 'I was always suspicious when he started hanging around here. But she trusted him. He used to take her to those student dances. She thought the sun shone out of his backside. But you can't trust them.'

'When was that?'

'About 1964. A couple of months before Christmas he turned up. Moss Side was different then. It was full of life.'

Shirley's eyes glowed with the memory of those days.

'He was all right really,' she said. 'A nice young boy. They used to laugh when they saw him. That class of white boy didn't use to come around here. But he didn't mind. It was his family. They'd never let him stop with one of us.'

'How did Roy find out his name?'

'I didn't know he had,' she said. 'This is the first I heard of it.'

'Did Roy ever talk about tracing his father? Anything like that?'

'Not till last year when he came back. They had him in the Scrubs. I didn't even know till he wrote me.'

A tear slid down one side of her face.

'Don't upset yourself, chuck,' I said quickly.

'I'm not.'

She shook her head firmly and wiped her eyes with a tissue. She was silent for a moment.

'When he came back he said he'd been thinking about it, and he wanted to know who he was. He'd always known that his father hadn't died like his mother said. I didn't tell him. I promised her on her dying bed. I didn't tell him.'

She paused and wiped her eyes again.

'I should have.'

'Never mind,' I said.

'He asked to look at the old photos, and he went and asked old Babatunde down the road. He was our cousin. He knew everything. He said he didn't tell him, but you can't trust people. I came back one day and he'd smashed my drawer open. He left it just like that. That was the last I saw of him.'

She got up quickly and left the room. I thought she'd gone to compose herself, and I felt a pall of guilt and depression at poking about in the tatters of her past.

In a moment I heard her footsteps coming back down. She was holding out a piece of paper.

'Grace died in July of '75,' she said. 'Roy was ten and I'd just got the job in the hospital. I had an idea about sending him away to a boarding school. Get him out of here. So I wrote to Spence.'

'Spence?' I said.

'Spence Baker. That was short for Spencer. We called him Spence. He used to send her money, you know. Religiously. Every quarter. So I wrote to him.'

She gave me the paper. It was a short, neatly typed letter dated in August 1975.

'Dear Miss Akimbola,' I read. 'My husband has asked me to reply to your letter. As you know, my husband helped your sister through some difficult periods, because he remembered and was grateful for her kindness to him as a student. Since her death, however, our connection with your family has come to an end. Much as we sympathise, it would be impossible to reply

59

with the generosity we'd like to every request for money. As for your nephew, we wish him well for the future, and in later years my husband would be pleased to offer him any advice he can about his choice of career. But to be fair to you, I must point out that it is unwise to assume that my husband feels an obligation to your family, and it would be cruel to encourage your nephew in any expectations of the kind.'

The letter was signed 'Mrs T Baker'.

'I didn't write again,' Shirley said.

'Roy saw this letter?'

'He must have done. It was in the drawer.'

I sipped my tea. When I imagined Roy sitting there reading that letter I could hardly swallow.

'He was a lovely boy,' she said. 'Till the trouble started.'

'Do you know a friend of his named Ford?' I asked her.

She thought for a moment.

'No. There were some Fords near us in Wilmslow Road, but I didn't really know them.'

I nodded. There was no more to say. I wanted suddenly to get away from her, from the haunting eyes of the handsome little boy in the photos on the mantelpiece.

I thanked her and got up.

'If you see Roy,' she said, 'tell him his auntie is still here.'

Chapter 12

Outside the house the afternoon sun had sunk behind Hulme and as I walked towards the junction with Princess Road the concrete blocks were casting a giant shadow over Moss Lane.

Behind me someone called out my name.

'Samson.'

I looked around. A car had stopped a few yards away from me, and a woman in a nurse's uniform was looking out smiling. I searched through my memory desperately and found nothing. Then I recognised her.

'Ida,' I called out.

She nodded, smiling, and I went over.

'This is Samson, kids,' she said to the two girls in the back seat.

The older would be about fourteen, the younger twelve.

'Hi. You girls wouldn't remember me, but I used to hold you when you were babies.'

I winked at them and they giggled. By some feat of memory I remembered their names.

'Yvette and Ismay,' I said, pointing to the older and the younger one in turn.

They giggled again.

'How long are you here for?' Ida asked.

'I was thinking about going back tonight.'

'You can't do that,' she said firmly. 'Come on. Get in. I'll take you home for some dinner.'

That was about what I'd expect. Up here they prided themselves on their hospitality.

She lived in the same row. But she drew up at a different house. They'd given her a larger one with three bedrooms. We went in and I sat around the kitchen table with the children while they had their tea.

Afterwards she said she had to take them to the youth centre to play netball. 'I'll be back in a half hour,' she said.

While she was gone I looked around. In the corner of the sitting room was a colour TV, and there was another small one in what looked like Ida's bedroom. There was the usual stereo and the familiar records, Bob Marley, Big Youth, Stevie Wonder, Diana Ross, Millie Jackson.

In the kitchen was a washing machine and a large blender. Ida was doing all right.

When she came back she bustled around, talking all the time.

'We can go out later,' she said. 'Take a walk round the pubs.'

'What about the kids?'

'Mum will have them.'

Her mother lived in the next street.

'Can we go down to Moss Side?' We were now in Longsight. 'I want to try and see some of my old spas. Something I want to find out.'

'Anything,' she said. 'But I can't stay too long.'

I told her why I had come to Manchester. She knew the Akimbolas by sight, but she couldn't tell me anything about Roy.

'That poor woman,' she said.

I couldn't tell whether she meant Grace or Shirley, and I supposed it didn't matter.

Later on we went to a Chinese restaurant. Afterwards we took a taxi to a club in Princess Road, a vestige of the old Moss Side, and my old stamping ground.

My favourite place had been a huge shebeen down the end of the road near Alexandra Park gates, which featured all-night stripping. The DJ played dub, the latest from Jamaica, a heavy bass line which vibrated through the floor and out of the top of your head, floating away in a haze of weed. Through the mist drifted the hard men of the area. Scarface, Big Willie, African Joe.

There was fighting most nights, and a trail of blood on the

pavement. Outside the park gates were lines of prostitutes, who from time to time would pop into the club for a break.

The sound and feel of the place spelled danger, chaos; and that must have been, I thought, the way that Spence Baker had seen it, the excitement of the forbidden clutching at his throat and pounding in his veins.

The old shebeen was gone now, with only a yard full of rubbish in its place, and the street looked bare and deserted. As we crossed Princess Road, Ida took my arm and squeezed it.

'I hate this place,' she said. 'Do we have to go?'

'I want to ask about something,' I told her. 'As soon as I see someone I can ask, we'll leave.'

The club looked plusher than when I'd last seen it. It was a large room on the ground floor with a bar and a billiard table. There were two smaller rooms upstairs where there was dancing. Half an hour before midnight it was crowded. Mostly men, the youngest in their twenties, the oldest balding fifty-year-olds. This was a watering hole for people of substance.

Jake was sitting near the back wall, beyond the bar, flanked by two teenage girls, both blondes, who wore short skirts and mesh stockings and looked almost identical. He was wearing a grey silk suit and a striped silk tie, and under the clothes he looked as fit and powerful as he always had.

'Clark Kent,' he said. 'What's happening?'

He didn't seem surprised to see me. Ida didn't greet him. Although she was still hanging on to my arm she glanced around the club, not looking at Jake. I disengaged myself from her and shook his hand.

'Want to see you, Jake.'

'Sit down,' he said.

He ignored the girls. He didn't look at Ida either.

Jake was the sort of man she warned her girls against. I had first met him when we were both middle order batsmen for the Princess Road Jesters. We had got together to play the police team, and after we'd thrashed them without mercy, we played the best teams in the city. Even Clive Lloyd came to watch us a couple of times. Jake was one of the best, always cheerful and encouraging, a great slips fielder.

It was nearly six months before I discovered he was a pimp who pushed weed on the side.

'Let's take a drink. To celebrate.'

Ida gave me a hard look, but I pushed her gently into the seat Jake vacated and struggled my way to the bar beside him.

'Give the girls what they drinking,' he said to the barman, 'and the same for the lady there with them.'

The barman put two whiskies in front of us without asking and went away. Jake looked round at me.

'What's happening?' I said.

He smiled. 'As you see. The usual. No better. No worse. You must come out to the house and see the family. My son's in music school now. Playing the violin.'

His wife, Sheena, was a mature version of one of the blondes, and they lived in a bungalow in Wythenshawe with a huge back garden where Jake had barbecues on Sundays for his respectable friends. I wondered what the neighbours thought he did.

'You know a youth named Akimbola, Jake? Roy Akimbola?'

Jake thought for a moment and then nodded. 'Just a youth,' he said. 'He used to hang around with some bad boys though. A few years back they did some things with shotguns. Garages and supermarkets. Most of them they didn't catch, but he went away with another one.'

'Ford?'

'That was it. A big bull. He used to box, but shotguns was quicker.' He shook his head sadly. 'Akimbola didn't really know the score. Ford was easy to spot, and easy to identify. By the time the police came breaking down doors most of the other guys were in Birmingham or London, one or two went to the Continent. Those two were still round here playing big men.' He chuckled with contempt.

I looked around. Ida was chatting animatedly with the two blondes.

'I've got to go,' I told Jake. 'I'm only here for tonight.'

He nodded. 'Next time. Let me know.'

We shook hands and I waved at Ida. She got up and came towards me, passing Jake without speaking.

In the car I asked her about the two girls.

'One is from Scotland,' she said. 'She came down here to be a nurse and packed it in. The other one is from Salford. They want to be models.'

'Models? What about Jake?'

'He's their manager. He's helping them with their photographs and getting them contacts.'

She looked sideways at me and we both burst out laughing.

'It's not funny,' she said. 'I hate that man. I don't know what you see in him.'

I shrugged. I liked Jake before I knew what he did, and I liked him afterwards. In a time and place where everyone was exploiter or exploited, pathetic or vicious, Jake had the unhurried elegance and fascination of a cruising shark.

'He is what he is,' I said. 'He's got no pretences.'

'You black men,' she said. 'You treat women like pigs.'

'Okay,' I said. 'He's a bad man. He should have been an IBM executive or a doctor or something real good like that. We're all hanging by our fingernails. Know what I mean?'

I'd expected an angry answer, but her mood changed suddenly.

'When are we going to progress?' she said reflectively. 'I don't know.'

The house was dark and silent.

'What about the kids?'

'My mum's keeping them,' she said.

I told her I'd be going first thing in the morning, and she said that she had to be in the hospital by six.

I'd be in London before lunchtime, I thought, and I'd go and see the Bakers during the day.

Now I knew more about Roy the signs pointed back in their direction, and this time they wouldn't fob me off with bullshit. Sitting on Ida's sofa my fists clenched in anger and my face tightened involuntarily when I thought of the Bakers.

'I'm going to bed,' Ida said.

I got up and followed her up the stairs, and we climbed into bed in a companionable silence.

Chapter 13

I got off the train with the feeling I always had coming back into the country from abroad. The city was waiting there for me, like a book that hadn't been opened for a long time. I had only been gone a day, and yet I felt as if I were renewing my acquaintance with London after a long absence. But when I walked out through the courtyard in front of Euston Station the sky was covered with bluish grey clouds, and there was a slight drizzle.

It was a damp, dark day with an ugly, foreboding feel.

I rang the Bakers as soon as I got in. Tess answered. When I said who I was she sounded surprised in a distant way.

'What can I do for you?'

'I'd like to speak to you and Mr Baker,' I said, 'or either of you. I think it's important.'

'I'm afraid we can't,' she said. 'In any case there really isn't any more to say. The crisis is over.'

She gave a strained little laugh.

'I don't think so,' I said. 'I really do need to speak to you.'

'I'll be blunt with you, Mr Dean,' Tess said. 'I don't think that we have anything more to say to each other and I'd be grateful if you stopped ringing.'

She put the phone down. I listened to the tone for a few seconds, then I rang Pete. When he answered I asked him whether Baker was in.

'Yes. I just talked to him.'

'Can I speak to him?'

'Sure. I'll put you through to his secretary.'

I waited for half a minute while the phone clicked and buzzed, then Baker's secretary came on the line. I told her who I was.

'Can I speak to the boss?'

'He's a bit busy right now. But I'll try him.'

After a few seconds of silence she came back on and said that he was busy and if I left a number she would get him to ring me. I gave her the number and put the phone down.

Out of the corner of my eye I caught the beginning of the lunchtime news.

I had turned the sound down on the television before I picked up the phone so that when the burning buildings and sprawled bodies came on the screen I didn't know where it was. It could have been anywhere, Africa, Asia, Latin America, or Britain itself. My hand reached out to turn up the volume, then I left it. Just for the moment I didn't want to know who was suffering.

After fifteen minutes or so, I rang Baker's office again.

'He's gone out I'm afraid,' his secretary said. 'I gave him your message but he's got a meeting and had to leave.'

'Can I reach him later?'

'No. He's got another meeting in the evening, and he's off to the constituency tomorrow. Can I make you an appointment for next week?'

I thanked her and said I'd get in touch in a few days.

I rang Pete again.

'Pete. The man is ducking me.'

'Ah huh.' Pete was noncommittal.

I guessed that he wished he could wash his hands of the whole affair.

'Other things have happened. I know a lot more about the matters we spoke about in Clapham. I must see him. For everyone's sake.'

There was a short silence on the line.

'Try his home late,' Pete said. 'He's got some kind of dinner on, but he'll spend the night at home before we go up to the constituency.'

'That's the best you can do?'

' 'Fraid so.'

'Thanks.'

'I didn't say a thing.'

I paced up and down trying to work out what to do. I had to see Baker. If Roy had been in touch with him last year, and the same Roy had been Virginia's friend, then she must have discussed him with her parents and they must have known exactly who he was.

I walked into the kitchen, sat down and got up again. More space. I needed more space. I ran down the stairs, walked down to Harrow Road and bought a local paper at the newsagent's opposite the police station at Paddington Green.

On the second page was a report of the two deaths. The cause of death was thought to be a heroin overdose. I didn't believe that either. Committed and intelligent junkies like Dick and Sally knew a lot about the effects of the drug, especially on themselves. They would know what to do if they noticed the symptoms of an overdose, and there were the emergency services if they were really desperate. One of them on their own might have blown it, but both of them together was different.

My suspicion was that the big man who had hit me had also given them the overdose and stopped them from using the phone till it was too late. He couldn't have been there by accident, either, clearing out the flat and taking Virginia's personal things.

Virginia had to be involved, and that meant that when her parents stopped me going after her, they were covering up something important. I had the feeling that the Baker family was caught up in a current of events they couldn't control. Everything to do with Roy had been tidied away, as if he were something you could press into a smelly dustbin. Perhaps the lid was about to come off, but I had the irrational desire to get Roy out of it. To make it all right.

Looking through the local paper made me remember how much I disliked them, a feeling that remained from my childhood, when every local paper I'd seen read like a racist tract. I tossed it away and kept on walking down the Harrow Road towards where Roy used to live. If he'd been a customer in one of the neighbourhood bookies, he might have left traces.

There were five within a hundred-yard radius of his former address, and I started with the largest one.

I struck gold right away.

Not that in other circumstances I would have said the Boss was gold, but as soon as I saw him I realised that my search would be easier. If Roy had been in any of these shops regularly, the Boss would know him.

I called out, 'Boss.'

He turned to face me and I saw that he had 'BOSS' printed on his sweater in big, red letters.

'Mr Dean,' he said. 'I don't want to see you. You always writing about people, all kinds of people except me.'

Back in the late sixties the Boss had been a ska singer. On stage he wore Bermuda shorts and banged himself on the head with a tea-tray. Since then he had lost his popularity, although some people remembered him with affection and nostalgia, and he was always talking about his comeback.

'Boss,' I said. 'I don't write about musicians any more.'

'Why don't you start again?'

'No more,' I told him. 'I hate you big-headed buggers.'

He laughed and gripped me in a bearhug. 'What you doing here?'

'Just looking around.'

'It's lucky you came today. I just finished recording my latest song.'

He held up a cassette and tapped the Sony Walkman he had round his neck. I sighed and took it from him.

The record was a soupy number about how much he missed his baby.

'Great,' I said when it was finished.

'I'm trying to get air-plays. They definitely promised me a play on Radio London. You know those guys. Help me out, nah?'

I nodded. I said I would help him out.

He slapped his hand into mine.

'Righteous.'

'Boss,' I said. 'You know a little mixed-race guy came around here? Name of Roy. With a big, muscular West Indian guy. Used to be a boxer.'

He frowned.

'With Northern accents. Manchester.'

His face cleared up. 'Oh yes. I seen them.'

'You know where they live?'

'Round here somewhere. I don't know where these guys live. Come on.'

'Boss. It's important. How can I find out?'

'I don't know,' he said thoughtfully. 'I don't really want to mess with those people. The big one is an animal. You know. Muscles in his head, man.'

'I'll be careful. How can I find out?'

He thought for a few seconds.

'I saw him down the Palm Grove a couple of times. If he's a member they would have some kind of address. I can find out.'

The Boss sang at the Palm Grove once or twice a week. 'To keep his hand in.'

'Let's go,' I said.

'Are you kidding, man? Number one they won't be open. Number two I still got some horses running. You know what I mean?'

I'd forgotten. Serious punters spent all day in the bookie shop, checking the starting prices before they bet and trying to latch on to the flow of the results. Some days all the favourites would win. Some days there'd be soft going at the racecourses and some unexpected results would turn up.

Horses who loved running in the mud would come up at twenty or thirty-three to one. Some days jockeys like Willie Carson couldn't lose. You had to stay with the action.

'Pick me up later,' he said, 'about half past eight.'

I was going to argue about it, but just then the next race started, and his eyes drifted away from me towards the board on which the lists of runners were pinned up. He made a fist and jerked it up and down, urging his horse on. I waited to hear the result.

On the other side of the room a well-dressed man who looked like an Italian or perhaps Maltese, shouted the name of his horse at the top of his voice and screamed a long hoarse scream when it came in first. He waved his betting slip in the air and began showing it to the people near him. There was a chorus of yells and hisses and cries of 'shut up', which he ignored. The Boss groaned loudly.

'Carson,' he said. 'Carson let me down again.'

A typical punter, he talked about jockeys as if he had a personal contract with them.

70

A short stocky Rasta, with a white cap on his head, his locks hanging down round his face, came up and gripped the Boss by the arm.

'Boss,' he said. 'Me tell you bet on the little American bwoy.'

'I'll see you later, Boss,' I said.

I walked slowly back through the afternoon sunshine. There wasn't much I could do till later. I felt tired and cold, needing the warmth of the sun, and I loitered as I went.

I kept on going past betting shops. Whenever I took notice it always seemed that poor districts had the most betting shops. But all the people who used them, especially the heaviest punters, knew that fortunes were being made from clients who had practically nothing themselves.

Every day in the bookie's you could hear men lecturing anyone who would listen about the futility of gambling. 'Why do we do it?' they would mutter. 'How can you win?' they would groan. But they kept coming back.

Back in Edgware Road I went into another betting shop to look at the latest results. Beside me were a group of teenagers, three boys and a girl, all holding bottles of wine or cans of beer. There was a hostel nearby and these groups of alcoholic kids had started appearing in the last few months. They looked exactly like the staggering old men who bedded down in Charing Cross and Camden Town, and when you looked beyond the tattered old overcoats and matted hair, it was a shock to see how young they were.

They smelled appalling too. Stale beer, vomit and urine.

I shifted my position, and I had just moved a few yards away when an Arab holding a plastic bag of shopping came in and started shouting.

'I have marked you all for salvation,' he shouted at the top of his voice. 'God sees all, and when I return I shall choose you. You are all marked.'

He pointed round the shop, stabbing out his finger at everyone in turn.

'Piss off,' someone said, but most people ignored him.

There was something creepy about the performance. Not so much as an individual turn, but because it seemed practically impossible these days to walk any distance through the centre of

71

London without meeting someone crazy, or a flurry of violence or a drunken teenager with vague distracted eyes.

Earlier in the century visitors to London used to remark on the undersized, twisted physiques of the poor. Today poverty in the city was linked with an aura of madness, violence and rage.

In the flat I rang Sophie. When she came on the line her voice sounded cheerful and untroubled.

'Has Virginia turned up at college by any chance?'

'No. No one's seen her for weeks.'

I asked her about herself. It was hard to end the conversation after a while. Looking for Virginia made me feel solitary and adrift, a wanderer picking through a rag bag of unpleasant memories. Sophie had unpleasant memories too, but along with them she had a kind of normality about her that reassured me.

I told her I'd get in touch over the weekend. I hoped.

Chapter 14

I woke up with a start when my watch chirped eight o'clock.
The dull day had turned into a dull and windy evening, and the
groups of robed Arabs along Edgware Road looked like clumps
of migrating birds who had arrived too soon.

The Boss emerged almost immediately when I rang the
doorbell.

'I have to leave early,' he said importantly. 'I'm going to pick
up a poosee later.'

'My business won't take long.'

He was dressed in a cream-coloured suit and a red silk shirt.
Round his neck was a fine gold chain strung through a tiny gold
watch which reversed to show a compass. There was a gold
identity bracelet round one wrist, and about five gold rings on
his fingers.

'You look like a walking jewellery shop, man.'

He accepted the compliment with a smug look. 'Chah man.
This is just normal.'

The Palm Grove was behind Oxford Street on the Selfridges
side. Inside it looked like a large pub lounge with a bar along
one side, a small stage at the other, and a dance floor about
twenty feet across, surrounded by clusters of small tables and
chairs.

'Go and find out,' I told the Boss. I knew I'd never get him
away if he got to the bar. 'I'll get you a drink and wait.'

He looked around, then disappeared in the direction of the

office. I crossed to the bar as unobtrusively as possible. Social manners among West Indians look breezy and informal to outsiders. In practice they are elaborate and ritualistic, and if I met people I knew it would take a long time to get away. Besides I was too depressed and confused to want to talk about myself.

Nearly everyone in the club was black. The women, mostly young, wore backless dresses and carefully fashionable outfits. Unlike the previous decade, Afros were out and so were the beaded locks that came after. Black women had begun to straighten and curl their hair again, and the hairstyles were a weird mixture of European and African, with the odd square-cut Grace Jones tuft sticking out.

This was one of those clubs where people with spare cash came to spend it, and to be seen doing so. Others came to be in the swim, to be part of where it was at.

A soul number was coming through the speakers and a few couples were embracing each other and moving slowly on the dance floor. Later on there wouldn't be room to move but it was too early for real action.

'Samson Dean,' a voice said and someone slapped me on the back.

I turned round and saw Len and Earl.

They managed a company which ran a photograph agency and sold beauty products for black people, but which had actually been set up to launder Nigerian money. They were wearing the obligatory silk suits and alligator shoes. Respectable businessmen, they also wore silk ties.

They asked me how I was.

'Not as cute as you boys,' I said.

'Trying to change your image?' Len asked. 'This is not a club for radicals.'

The girls with them looked at me curiously. They seemed to be models of some sort, all about nineteen or twenty years old. They wore short skirts, patterned stockings, and were decorated with bits of net and shiny earrings, making up a striking little group at which the men in the club stared covertly.

I guessed they were the sort of pretty, naive kids who came out of the contests which went along with the grass roots beauty trade. Short of impossible targets like TV presenters and big-time singers, these were the ultimate status symbols for businessmen like Len and Earl.

'Still running errands for crooked Nigerians?' I asked them.

'Intellectual,' Len said. 'Bourgeois intellectual.' He made the words sound like an obscene insult. He turned to the girls. 'This is Sammy Dean. He's an intellectual. Always writing about black people in the white man newspaper.'

As schoolboys we had taken up black militancy at the same time. When Len went into the Panthers I had joined the Black Unity and Freedom Party, and we'd spent more time fighting each other than anyone else.

Time had made those arguments irrelevant, but Len still liked to have a sly dig whenever we met. In addition I had gone to university and he hadn't. He liked me to know how well he was doing.

'What about your Nigerian money man, though?' I said. 'What I hear is that the government is freezing foreign assets. But I suppose your money is well into Swiss bank accounts by now.'

Len grinned and rolled his eyes at the girls.

'Blood,' Earl said. 'You're the type that's always running down your fellow black businessmen.'

'Oh no,' I said. 'I like to see you get on. What frightens me is that one day they'll find you boxed up in a crate at London airport. Next year this time some African hit man could be walking round wearing alligator shoes. You know what I mean?'

Earl shook his head and turned away from the bar. 'Let's go, girls.'

He walked towards a table in the corner, ushering the girls in front of him. Len stayed where he was, grinning at me.

'How are things?' he said.

I shrugged. He used to wear his hair in a bushy Afro, but now it was twisted into the greasy ringlets of the Hollywood curl. Even so I could see the odd strand of white above his forehead.

'Not bad,' I said. 'How about you?'

'Good,' he said. 'Real good. The company's doing well.' He made a little gesture with his fist. 'Things have changed.'

Len was right. Things had changed. I was out looking for a

Tory politician's daughter and he was wearing alligator shoes. Not bad.

'How's the wife and children?'

'Okay.'

He took out his wallet and handed me a picture of his family. I said they looked great and showed him a picture of my son. He gave it back to me and squeezed my arm.

'Later.'

He patted me again and went off towards the table in the corner. He sat down and put his arm round one of the girls.

I looked round and saw the Boss coming.

'All right,' he said. 'They didn't have an address, but one of the girls knows where he lives. She lives nearby.'

'Good. Where is it?'

'Well. She don't exactly know the address, but she can direct you. Down Kilburn.' He pointed out one of the girls waiting at the tables, waved at her and she came over.

'It's about that guy,' the Boss said. 'The thing that walks like a a man.'

'Winston,' she said.

'That's right,' the Boss said. He was clowning slightly for the girl's benefit. She was tall and shapely, with an expression that was both demure and experienced. 'The Boss wants to know where the man lives.'

'I don't know the address but I've seen him going down a street off Kilburn High Road.'

She told me where it was and went away without looking back.

'Yes,' the Boss said. 'I like that little poosee. Nice.'

'Okay Boss,' I said. 'I owe you one.'

'Why don't you give it to me now?' he said. 'Just a ten would do.'

He laid his hand open on the bar. 'Just slip it in my hand.'

I slipped it. He crumpled it up and put it in his pocket without looking. Then he made a little bye-bye gesture with his fingers and walked away.

'Later,' I said, but he didn't turn around.

Chapter 15

I drove directly to the street the girl had described. It was still about an hour short of closing time, and there was a busy traffic on the pavements along Kilburn High Road.

I turned off the main road after the railway arch. The house was on the right hand side, she had said, not too far from the corner, but she didn't know which it was. He could be living at any one of about twenty in the row of terraced houses.

I parked, got out and began checking the names on the doors. No Winston. I went back to the car. I had nothing to do. I might as well wait, I thought.

I walked back to the High Road for a takeaway. For a moment, I thought about going into one of the pubs for a quick drink, but at this hour, just before closing time, the idea didn't appeal.

The last time I'd been in one of these pubs was at lunchtime. A small pipe band, children in brightly coloured kilts, had been playing, and around them a large group of men were singing, one of those Irish songs which sounded both mournful and angry. As I sat down one of the little girls had approached me shaking a collecting tin.

I was reluctant, but the vibration of suppressed violence in the air and the flushed angry faces of the men round me, made me feel it was a good idea to contribute.

In the main road I looked around. During my schooldays, going home from the pictures at this time of night, the only places open would be fish and chip shops. Now from where I was standing I could choose from a Chinese takeaway, three kebab shops, five Indian tandoori joints, and a number of groceries.

Back in the car, the street where I'd parked was silent, almost deserted. Two teenage girls came along, their high heels rapping sharply on the pavement, and crossed to the other side when they saw me sitting there. After them was a middle-aged man, shepherding two small girls, too young to be out so late, wearing elaborate dresses of satin and organdie, and some sort of tiaras on their heads. In a little while they were followed by a couple absorbed in each other.

A few cars came by and parked further down, breaking the silence with the sound of doors slamming. No one very big. No one even remotely resembling the description of Winston Ford.

About half past eleven a familiar custom car rolled past me and stopped a few doors down on the other side.

I slumped back in my seat as the man who had bashed me in Notting Hill got out.

He was big, and now that I had a chance to take a good look at him I could see that he was a lot bigger than I had realised that night. He moved like a man who was conscious that he could beat the shit out of most people he encountered. Watching him I resolved that I wouldn't tangle with this man again unless I had a weapon in my hand.

I slumped right down so that he wouldn't see me, but he went into the house without a backward glance. It was about half an hour before he came out again. I had been afraid that he was settled for the night, but it was early, and that was unlikely, so I waited.

I felt a mixture of excitement and fear. This had to be Winston, and he had to be involved with Roy and Virginia and whatever was going on. In any case he could lead me to them.

When he came out he had changed his clothes. He'd been wearing a woolly hat and a donkey jacket, but now he was dressed in his three-piece suit, topped off by a broad-brimmed black hat.

He made a three-point turn and I had to wait until he went round the corner before I could turn and follow him, but it was easy to pick him up going back down Kilburn High Road. The lights in his back window glowed invitingly, like a sign.

He turned left and went up towards Swiss Cottage instead of the other way to Paddington. From there we went past Hampstead Heath and the pond.

The glowing red lights speeded up as we went through the empty stretch of road past Spaniards Inn, and we turned left again before Highgate.

The houses on either side of the road had been looking more and more prosperous since we'd approached Swiss Cottage, but now we were passing buildings which were ostentatiously wealthy.

Going along behind Winston I wondered what kind of life he and Roy had in mind when they went out with their shotguns. Some of these houses were owned by men who had literally stolen millions, and they'd done it, most of them, by far more complex, less honest means. It was only some kinds of crime which didn't pay.

In a mile or so we were through the belt of money between Hampstead and Muswell Hill, and speeding down the hill on which Alexandra Palace was built. Hornsey. I thought we were going to Tottenham but at the bottom of the hill, before we reached Turnpike Lane, the lights turned left into a side street of narrow terraced houses and stopped. Taken by surprise I continued past the place where he'd parked and drove round the corner.

I parked quickly and ran back, but by then Winston had disappeared and there was no one in sight. I clenched my fists in frustration.

I couldn't sit round the corner in the car in case he came out again. If this was where Roy and Virginia were hiding out I had to know which house it was.

About twenty minutes went by while I leaned on the wall cursing my fate. I seemed to have been chasing round a wilderness of streets for longer than I could remember. I had no way of telling when this would end, and I felt nothing but tiredness and depression.

In a street close by, the round shape of a gasometer outlined in winking red lights reared up against the sky. In the silence and the dark it seemed to loom threateningly, and I looked round quickly a couple of times with the feeling that there was someone coming up behind me. I was wearing a shirt and a pullover, but the night had turned chilly and I rubbed my arms to keep the circulation going.

Standing there I longed for lights and noise or the white scorching heat of a tropical noon.

It seemed longer but it was only half an hour before Winston came out, followed by another man. I strained to see whether I could identify Roy, but at that distance I couldn't tell who he was. I noted the house, and ran for my car as they crossed the pavement. I got in just in time to crouch down below the steering wheel till I heard them go past.

I waited again for the red rear lights to disappear round the corner, then the engine didn't start first go, so there was nothing in sight when I got back to the main road and the junction between the roads that led on the right back to Muswell Hill, on the left to Tottenham, and straight on towards Camden Town and the West End.

The lights were against me, so I stopped and craned my neck right and left, listening for the rasping sound of Winston's engine, but I couldn't make it out among the other sounds. I couldn't see the red glow either, and I thought they might be hidden by the curve of the road ahead, so I took a chance and went up towards the centre of London when the lights changed.

I held the speed down till I was past the police station, then pelted through Hornsey as fast as I dared, but I didn't catch up with Winston. When I reached Camden Town I gave up the chase. From that point there were too many possibilities.

I thought of going back to the house Winston had just left, but I didn't know who lived there and even if Roy and Virginia were around, I suspected that I ought to approach them more carefully. Next day would be better. But I had to know more. That meant I couldn't leave Baker till next day. In any case he'd be going out of town and I couldn't afford to wait.

A suspicion was beginning to form in my mind about Roy and Winston. The younger man might be working out some plot or fantasy which connected him to the man he thought was his father. But Winston needed money to drive the custom car, to buy new suits and be a big man at places like the Palm Grove, and perhaps his imagination didn't end with rivalling people like Len and Earl.

We had driven through some of the richest real estate in the country on the way from Hampstead, and it was possible the choice of route said something about Winston's dreams and desires.

But what he wanted seemed straightforward and direct. Roy's motives had to be more complicated and devious, and everything I'd heard about him had the flavour of a kid who was being towed along in his confusion by a stronger, more forceful character.

There could be a point coming up when the interests of the two men would go in different directions, and if there was a clash between them my money would be on Winston.

Chapter 16

By the time I got to Wandsworth Road it was gone one o'clock. I sat outside the darkened house getting up the resolve or whatever it was I needed to go and ring on Baker's bell. Eventually I realised that I'd been sitting there for nearly ten minutes, and I got up and crossed the pavement to the door.

I had thought, at first, that they must be in bed, but when I rang the bell a faint gleam appeared behind the glass panel at the top of the door. In a moment it opened and Baker appeared. He was wearing a cardigan and an angry frown.

'This is intolerable,' he said. 'I don't know what you want and I don't care. If you want to see me please make an appointment with my secretary.'

He made to slam the door but I stuck my foot in the opening.

'I've just come from Manchester,' I said, 'and I've been hearing all about good old Spence Baker. From Shirley. Shirley Akimbola? You remember her. She sends her regards.'

He said nothing for a moment. He simply stood there staring at me.

The light from the street lamp had a slightly distorting effect on colour, but even so I could see that the blood had drained from his face, turning it from an indignant red to gleaming fish-belly white.

'Can I come in?' I said. 'I tried to get you all morning in your office, but you were unavailable, and you're going away tomorrow. I'm really sorry to disturb you so late but I think it's absolutely essential that I talk to you.'

He stood aside slowly like a man in a dream.

'Come in.'

I walked in and went into the big downstairs room I'd been in before. At the further end a lamp was casting a dim light towards the floor. Two armchairs were arranged at a slight angle so that they faced the window. Tess was sitting in one of them looking back at us as we entered the room. Next to her on a small table was a bottle of whisky and a couple of glasses. The effect was one of private and cosy intimacy.

She turned her head away when she saw me and went back to staring out of the window. There was a light out there, near the rosebed, and it gave the scene that green fairyland look that you get from the glow of light through leaves at night.

Baker pulled a straight chair up to where they were sitting.

'Sit down please.'

I sat down. He lowered himself back into the armchair and without asking, picked up a glass and poured me a drink. I took it without bothering about the polite noises. I felt as if somehow we had come to the end of a long road to confront each other, and it was as if we were old opponents warily gathering strength for what was coming.

'You wanted to speak to me,' he said. He hesitated. 'About Manchester.'

It was odd. Talking like this, not trying to convince me of anything, he sounded bored and faintly disdainful. I didn't think it was deliberate. That was just how he sounded.

As I began to speak I watched him carefully, half expecting him to signal his wife in some way, but he didn't move or look at her.

'I mentioned Manchester,' I said, 'because I've just come from there. I met a lady named Shirley Akimbola who said you were her nephew's father. This nephew is the same boy who's been hanging around with Virginia. He calls himself Roy Baker, by the way.'

If I was hoping for a big reaction I didn't get one. Tess turned a little to look at Baker, but he merely raised his glass to his lips and sipped, in exactly the same way as he had been doing before.

'I know he was here a year ago, and I think when he got out of prison this year he probably contacted your daughter somehow and told her his story. I think that if he did, she must have asked you about it, and if she did, then you knew who the black boy was all the time, and her disappearance was part of a family affair which you decided not to tell me about. But I also think that something happened which made you want me to stop looking for them. At first I thought it might be some scandal about which you were being careful, but now I think it might be more serious, and I thought that if you could tell me more about what's actually going on I could help. I mean I know enough to put the cat among the pigeons if I wanted to, but I don't.'

Baker said nothing, instead he raised his glass and took another small sip. Tess was still staring at him, as she had been all the time I was speaking. From where I sat I could only see her in three-quarter profile, and her forehead was creased, but not in anger. Her expression as she gazed at him was perplexed and curious as if she was trying to work out the answer to some puzzle.

I tried again.

'I didn't believe that Virginia was staying with a friend in the country, and in the circumstances I thought that you were either trying to be insulting or you assumed I was stupid. But the first was unlikely for a politician, and the second was impossible because you're not stupid yourselves. I came to the conclusion that you were too panicked and upset to care that it was such a naff story.'

'Or perhaps we thought it was absolutely none of your business,' Tess said. Her tone was preoccupied, abstracted.

'You're probably right,' I said. 'I'm not here because I care that much about Virginia or you. No. I think your daughter, being who she is, if she survives, will most likely put all this behind her. It's Roy I'm worried about. See, I've got this little boy who's mixed, like him, and I suppose I've got them confused somehow, but I kept thinking about Roy being desperate and lonely and getting deeper and deeper into some kind of trouble he'd never get out of.'

Baker stirred, and I stopped. All of a sudden it seemed important to tell them how I really felt, to open my thoughts, as if that was the only way I could get through. I didn't know what I was saying but I opened my mouth and let it happen.

'That's not it,' I said. 'That's what I feel now. No. At the beginning it was really something about people like you and people like me. What we are affects each other, but there's a big blank space between here where I am and there where you are, and no one can describe it or talk clearly about it, even though we know just what it is. Then Roy was there somewhere in the middle, like the answer to this big puzzle, with all these mysterious hints about the past tied up in him, and feelings we could all feel. But no one would even admit to knowing who he was. I mean who're you kidding?'

My voice had risen and I'd almost shouted by the end. Tess put her hand to her face and pressed her fingertips lightly against her forehead.

'Grenville,' she said. Her voice sounded deeper and had about it something more than anger. 'Isn't this enough yet?'

Baker tensed his muscles as if about to get up, and he opened his mouth, but he still had an uncertain look about him, as if he knew he should get up and throw me out, but couldn't quite work himself up to it.

I held my hands up in a placatory gesture before he could speak.

'Please,' I said. 'Hear me out. There's not much more.'

Without waiting for his reaction I hurried on.

'Then I went to Manchester and found out more about him, and I thought he'd been betrayed and abandoned and treated like shit by his own father ever since he'd been conceived, and so that made me want even more to try and find him and sort this mess out. I don't have much to believe in but I'm a father too.'

'I congratulate you,' Baker said. 'But you're barking up the wrong tree. Yes. Manchester is true. No. I'm not the father that the boy's looking for.'

'How do you know? Shirley seemed pretty definite about it.'

'Grace knew other men. Quite a few.'

'Yes but how did you know that you were not the father?'

'Grace herself wasn't absolutely certain.'

He sipped his whisky and looked at me steadily.

There was a faint smile on his face, and it struck me that in spite of everything there was a trace of defiant delight and irrepressible male pride in the memory of his relationship with

85

Grace. The same thought must have occurred to Tess because her expression changed and she turned away sharply.

'You must have had substantial doubts,' I said, 'to keep on sending her money for the better part of ten years.'

He spread one hand in a noncommittal gesture. 'Perhaps.'

Tess shifted her weight in the chair and looked straight at me. Her features were set in a cold white mask out of which her eyes blazed in the dim light.

'My husband is extremely loyal. It makes him a soft touch. If I'd known about the money I'd have asked him to stop it sooner.'

The shadow of an old guilt crossed Baker's face. I suspected, in spite of his denials, that he believed Roy was his son. I suspected also that it was Tess who had put her foot down over the relationship.

'Shirley showed me your letter,' I told her. 'Roy saw it as well.'

Baker made a sound that was halfway between a sigh and a soft moan.

I glanced at him. All I had to go on were my own feelings as a father, because I had no way of telling what a man of his sort would feel, but I wondered how much it had cost him at the time to agree to the outright rejection.

'I thought it was wise to clarify the situation,' Tess said.

The situation was that Baker couldn't afford such reminders of his past. It was possible that matters might have fallen out differently if he hadn't been such a likely candidate for public office.

Listening to the hard tone of Tess's voice, it struck me that she had wanted his career as much or more than he did. The young man who had plunged so eagerly into the low life of Moss Side would probably have found it easier to let go of the dream of political power.

'I suppose it was your letter that brought Roy here last year.'

'Yes. That was unfortunate.'

The Bakers looked at each other, and for a moment their eyes locked together and held steady, then Tess looked away quickly. 'He turned up with some lunatic notion about being recognised as Grenville's son and heir.'

I grimaced. I didn't want to imagine that meeting.

'What did you tell him?'

'What I'd said in the letter. But he insisted on seeing Grenville, and he came back with a huge ugly man. We made him wait in the car.'

Baker moved but he didn't speak. Instead he poured another round, setting the bottle down carefully in the exact centre of the table. 'It was impossible to make him see reason. We had to resolve the situation.'

'By having him nicked?'

'No,' Tess said sharply. 'That was nothing to do with us. Our solicitor handled all that. His first concern was to keep us out of it, and of course we knew very little about what was happening.'

I could guess how that went. Send a few hard cops to make enquiries about two black youths like Roy and Winston, and you could write your own script.

'Did he come back recently?'

'No. We've heard nothing from him since. He wrote from prison, though. A horrid letter, blaming us for all his troubles and threatening revenge. I tore it up. That was the end of the affair.'

Except that it wasn't.

'Did Virginia mention meeting him?'

'I don't know, she might have said something. In any case we didn't connect the two things.'

'Didn't he tell her?'

Instead of replying she looked at Baker. 'It's very late.'

Baker looked at me.

'We've told you what we know. It doesn't much matter what you believe about where Virginia is. We're satisfied she's safe. As for Roy, I regret the entire episode. I regret that he was encouraged to behave as he did. I might have been able to help him if he'd approached me differently. But that was all a long time ago and it doesn't matter now. We wanted you to stop because there was no point in going on, and we would like to forget about the whole business. This was a mistake.'

His eyes bored into mine. They seemed to become a deeper shade of blue as I looked, closing round the dark spot in the middle.

'We've given you,' he paused and reached out to look at the small gold watch on Tess's wrist, 'over an hour. I've listened and I've talked to you, because you were kind enough to offer to help. But now we're tired and we'd like to bring all this to an end.'

He raised his eyebrows, inviting me to get up and leave.

'You know Virginia's flatmates are both dead?'

'They died of an overdose. Yes. It has nothing to do with our daughter, or anything else we've been discussing.'

'Don't be too sure,' I said. 'Your daughter is a junkie too, according to everyone who knows her.'

I told them everything that had happened in the last few days.

As I talked, I felt a sort of vicious triumph. I had earned every penny they'd given me, and unless I'd missed my guess, all this would give them a couple of very nasty moments. But when I caught myself thinking that, I felt a surge of guilt at the idea that this moment of revenge had been somewhere at the back of my mind all through the last few days. On the other hand, it was too late to stop.

'I'll tell you what I think,' I said. 'I think that if I was her father I'd be worried about her drug habit. And I'd be worried about her and Roy and Winston being mixed up in something together. Roy is one kind of problem, but Winston needs money and he doesn't care very much about how he gets it, and he likes handling guns and knocking people about. If I'm right your daughter is probably in real danger. But you know your own business best. If you're satisfied you've got it under control, that's fine. I came here with the idea that I might be able to help you. If I can't, I'll say goodnight.'

Now it was my turn to patronise them, I thought, and I got up, feeling the effect of the whiskies as I rose. Suddenly Baker put out his hand, almost touching me.

'Would you mind waiting in the kitchen?' he said. 'For a few minutes.'

I nodded and went out. They said nothing till I was out of the room, and through the door I could hear Tess speaking in a sharp, complaining tone. Then I went into the kitchen and sat down.

I felt as if I'd been awake for a week. I had the sensation I'd often had after a long jet flight, of seeing the world through glass.

88

I thought there was something nasty and curdled about the whole story and the Bakers' reaction to it. It was the way that time had transformed the relationship between Grace and Spence Baker into the impetus for a spiral of betrayal, violence and deceit. The original impulse on both sides must have been full of youthful curiosity and joy. But seen from this distance it was a picture framed in exploitation and racial contempt. This was Roy's heritage.

Half asleep now, I thought about Sophie and I found myself wondering whether her father had been a man like Baker, and about what had happened to her mother.

Baker and Tess came in and sat down. By coincidence we found ourselves in exactly the same positions round the table as we had been during our first meeting. It was as if we had scrubbed out everything between this time and that, and we were about to start again.

Baker leaned forward.

'I must have,' he said, 'your solemn word that you won't repeat anything I'm going to tell you, and your promise not to take any action unless we approve it first.'

I suppressed the impulse to giggle. It crossed my mind to hold up my fingers the way we used to in the Boy Scouts, but looking at his face I knew it was the wrong moment for humour. The ritual phrases sounded naive but they probably made it possible for him to tell me what he had to.

'I promise,' I said.

He stared at me seriously, then nodded.

'It started a few months ago. It may have been going on longer, but we first noticed that she kept falling asleep when she came home, and she looked different. Then we went to see her, and we saw her flatmates. They'd never been here and we didn't know anything about them till then. The next time my wife looked for marks on her arms. It was disgusting.'

His voice broke and he sat up in his chair. Tess had her elbow on the table and her hand covered her mouth.

'We confronted her and she said she had only been doing it for a short time. For fun. For fun. She said she could handle it. That's what they all say, isn't it?'

I shrugged.

'She said she would stop. I arranged treatment for her out of

89

London, and when she came back we thought it was all over, but she wouldn't leave the flat. We insisted and she was just about to move back home when she met Roy somehow. After that it was impossible. She kept on asking me about him. Accusing. He'd convinced her utterly, and from that time he seemed to have an enormous influence over her. We were certain she had started using the drug again, but she denied it. Every time we spoke she demanded that something should be done about Roy.'

As it lay on the table Baker's hand began to tremble. I watched it in fascination, and he noticed. He took it off the table and put it in his lap.

His face was haggard with the effort of talking about those times, when his daughter had come to lash him with the scorpions of buried guilt.

'Then one weekend she had arranged to meet her mother for lunch and she didn't turn up. We haven't seen or heard from her since.'

'Why didn't you want to keep on looking?'

'Something happened. The day before we spoke to you we got a letter saying that if we wanted to see Virginia alive again, we would pay into her bank account the sum of twenty thousand pounds.'

'You paid it?'

'No. We thought it was some kind of joke or trick she'd been talked into, and we thought that if we could find her we could clear the whole matter up. Then a few days later, we, Tess, that is, got a telephone call. The man said he would hurt her unless we paid the money over.'

'It was vile,' Tess said in a tight voice. 'He threatened unspeakable things if we didn't pay or if we called in the police. Virginia spoke to me just for a few seconds, then they cut her off and she began screaming. He said she screamed when she was hurt, and he said it would be a hundred times worse if we didn't pay.'

'Did you believe it? Paying money into the victim's bank account sounds a bit weird.'

'We thought so at first, but it would be different if she was in their power or in with them somehow.'

He gestured helplessly.

'We thought it might be a debt to some sort of pushers, and they wouldn't let her go until she'd paid.'

'So you paid it.'

'Yes. We were expecting her home today or looking for some kind of word. But tonight we got another phone call.'

'It was the same man,' Tess said, 'and he said they wanted fifty thousand in cash. If we didn't pay we'd never see her alive again. I tried to ask him if she was well but he wouldn't listen. He said he would be in touch again and not to contact the police, then rang off.'

'What are you going to do?'

'We were discussing it,' he said.

He looked at Tess and she looked away.

'What about the police?'

'No. Not yet,' Tess said quickly.

Baker sighed. 'It might be something Virginia's involved in. The threats may be meaningless. We were certain of it at first.'

'Why?'

'Twenty thousand is the exact amount of a legacy a cousin left her recently. It's in trust. She can't touch it for another five years. Fifty thousand is the amount her grandmother left her. All her money is tied up till she's older.'

'You think she's behind it all?'

'We don't know. We can't believe that. But it may not be an ordinary kidnapping. There may be certain difficulties in calling the police in right now.'

I understood. His daughter might wind up in jail and the newspapers would have a field day.

'But if she's in danger.' Tess paused, as if she was holding hysteria in check. 'We have to do something.'

'This man you mentioned. At the flat. Could he be something to do with it?'

I thought quickly. Winston had to be involved somehow and he was the only connection I could think of. Virginia could be anywhere, but I was sure that Roy would be with her or know what had happened, and Winston wouldn't be far away from Roy. If Virginia was in control it was hard to understand why she would make two demands for money, unless the first lot hadn't been enough. Perhaps the first one had been a test to see if it would work.

'He must be,' I said. 'There's no way of finding out. but he would be the one.'

I looked at Tess.

'If the man on the phone was Winston he would have to be with her or in contact with her at some point. You can put him off for a little while next time he rings by asking for proof. A voice on the telephone is no good. It could be a tape. Ask him for a picture with a newspaper showing the date. That will mean he has to see her.'

'How will that help?'

'I know where he lives, and I can follow him for a while, at least until the money is due to be paid. If it's not him then we don't lose anything.'

'It sounds like a risk even if it is this man,' Tess said. 'It might be better just to pay them now and sort it out when it's over.'

I looked at Baker.

'When you've paid over the money Virginia will be alone with two or more violent criminals and a big bag of dosh. You've already paid out something and she hasn't come back. You haven't called the police. Any course of action you take seems to me to be as risky as another.'

Baker nodded. 'I think you're right. We must do something.'

Tess made a sound like a gasp, but she said nothing.

'Did the man on the phone say when he'd ring again?'

'No.'

'I'll ring you tomorrow,' I said.

I was dropping. I could hardly keep my eyes open, and I needed to go home and get some sleep. I would have to be up and doing early.

On the way out I remembered something I'd meant to ask.

'What kind of car does Virginia have?'

'A red Golf.'

He gave me the licence number and I wrote it down.

At the door he shook my hand with a genuine warmth. 'Whatever happens,' he said, 'thank you.'

I nodded and turned away. I was too tired to react even with surprise, and everything I'd heard filled me with depression and dread.

I drove home in a dream, parked, and then walked round the corner to the all-night shop. As I approached it, a black youth with a lively jaunty air detached himself from a small group of loitering girls and came towards me.

'You want some sensemillia?' he said. 'Best you ever smoked man.'

I shook my head and kept on walking, into the shop. It was about four in the morning and there were several girls and a couple of youths hanging around in front of it. Up close the girls looked haggard and grubby. On the way back from the shop the boy who had spoken to me fell into step.

'Hey. You want some coke?'

I looked round at him. 'Will it change my life?' I said.

He laughed in high shrieking whoops.

'No,' he said, still chuckling. 'It won't change your life. For that you need something stronger.'

Chapter 17

The telephone rang, and I turned down the TV to answer it. I'd slept most of the morning away, and I still felt fuzzy and disorientated, but I recognised the voice of the Boss immediately.

'Pass by and see me later on,' he said. 'I got something for you.'

'Okay. What time?'

'This morning. As soon as.'

I put the phone down and went out. I got to the car just before the traffic warden, a short, pretty blonde, could put a ticket under the windscreen wipers.

As I drove off I nearly thumbed my nose at her, but a touch of shame stopped me. I waved instead, and she smiled brightly.

When I got to the Boss's flat he opened the door after the first ring, slapped his hand into mine, gripped the ends of my fingers and pulled, said 'Yeah,' and led the way into his room.

It contained a double bed, an armchair, a telephone and a cooker in an alcove behind a curtain. It seemed cramped, overcrowded and hot, even though the window was wide open.

'That big guy you asked me about,' he said. 'I heard something.'

I sat in the armchair.

'Tell me.'

'I didn't tell you nothing, right?'

'Right.'

'Listen. I need some more duns, you know. I got to go there tonight. Seek out this poosee.'

'Okay.'

'If I could hold twenty.'

'Okay Boss. Don't worry. You got it.'

Twenty was very fair if what he had to say was useful. 'Well,' he said slowly. 'You know my Apache friend.'

The Apache was a Ceylonese for whom the Boss acted as a go-between with Arabs and Nigerians who were shifting currency about. I nodded.

'Yes. I know the guy.'

'Well he's doing some business with coke and things like that you know. The currency business is a little bit funny right now.'

I knew. The international fixers who had their roots down here in the Boss's little deals had recently burned their fingers. Banks had collapsed. Huge sums had been frozen, and reforms in various countries had choked the usual channels. The confusion had begun to force diversification on some of the small men who depended on the big deals.

'So some people saw him a couple of weeks ago. A brother in Notting Hill introduced them. They wanted to part-finance a big deal.'

'And Winston was one of them?'

'No. My man is careful. He just puts money together, does the deal and takes a commission. He's a businessman. He wouldn't have got involved with that guy. He doesn't look like he's got that kind of money and he's too rough. No. It was the other one, the half-white.'

'You mean the mixed-race boy, Roy.'

'I don't care what you call him. He had a rich girlfriend, a junkie girl from good family. She had money. So they gave the Apache a couple of grand and he went ahead.'

'He sold it to them?'

'No. He don't work like that. He doesn't have anything to do with it. It's like import and export. Somebody was bringing some stuff in and needed an investment on this end. So the Apache and some other fellas put up the money and when the stuff comes in, they pass it on to other people. Then those people pass it to other people. There's no risk.'

'Sure. He's just a hard-working businessman. What happened?'

'They were supposed to hand over the money the other day,

and this big guy turned up with them. Like some kind of bodyguard. Well, the Apache don't dig rough stuff, and he didn't like that, but it didn't matter anyway. There was a little hitch. Some of the goods had got seized, and of course that put the price of the investment up. Sometimes it happens like that. You still make your money, you just have to put more in. So he explained it to them and told them that they had to find more money, and this big guy threatened him.'

'They wouldn't pay?'

'Well, they agreed to pay in the end, but the Apache didn't like that. I mean he's accustomed to dealing with international businessmen. Real big guys. Not this juvenile delinquent shit.'

The only problem was that the big guys sometimes ended up in jail halfway across the world.

'Now he's got to be careful. So when I mentioned you were looking for this guy, he wanted to know what was happening. You see this guy is crazy. He wants to deal for himself. Set up his own thing. So he's getting some of the stuff and going into business for himself.'

'He'll end up a millionaire.'

'No. He'll end up in shit up to his neck. He's changed the whole deal. Nobody's going to like that. Besides he's only got half the money and he wants something in his hand before he pays over the rest. The Apache don't work that way.'

'But he's going to do it.'

'He's got to. He don't intend to fool around with that guy.'

'They're doing it today?'

The Boss shrugged. 'I don't know. Probably.'

'So where will they do all this? At Goonay's house?'

'No. You crazy? You're joking. He wouldn't keep stuff at his house. Probably he'll get them to meet the people and do business somewhere else.'

I understood. Goonay, the Apache, was going to divorce himself from the whole business, and from Winston. If the Apache was spreading the news of Winston's deal around as well, it might mean that he wanted to sabotage it in some way. Perhaps I was meant to do something about it, but I didn't know what. I handed the Boss twenty.

'Right,' he said. 'You see the favours I do you? This is a big story?'

'It's not a story.'

'I could give you a real story about drugs, you know. Frontline. Handsworth. Everything. If you could get a newspaper to pay we could make some money. A hundred thousand. They would jump at it.'

I laughed. 'Do leave off, Boss. Even if you know everything, they wouldn't pay.'

He shrugged, smiling. 'Okay, you blood. You don't want to be rich.'

Driving down into Harrow Road I laughed out loud again, thinking about the Boss's proposition. Every time there was a riot two or three pushers would phone me offering to tell the story of their lives for publication, quoting sums up to half a million. Chequebook journalism was a golden legend among them.

Back in the flat I rang the Bakers. Tess answered.

'Any news?'

'No.'

She sounded tired and out of sorts.

'I'll ring later.'

I put the phone down and turned on the TV. The news was on and a politician was talking about unemployment. He was wearing a neat dark suit and gold-rimmed spectacles. I wondered whether he was thinking of people like the Boss or the kids I saw staggering about Edgware Road or the teenage prostitutes standing in line. Maybe he was, but I had the feeling that people of that kind weren't part of anything the politician had in mind.

Baker also lived at a distance from the world in which his daughter was now operating, and I guessed that he must have experienced the same sort of shock as a first-class passenger in a train crash. One minute travelling in luxury, the next minute suddenly catapulted into a horror of screaming metal, blood and pain.

I slept until the canned laughter woke me. On the screen three women were jumping up and down, squealing. I lay still, watching without understanding.

Chapter 18

At about nine I was sitting in the car opposite the Apache's house. The windows were dark and it was obvious that there was no one at home. The thought of another long futile wait crawled in my brain like a wounded rat.

Being in that road made things worse. It was a street which ran diagonally up to Clissold Park, on the border between Islington and Stoke Newington. As a boy I had walked there often, going to meet my mother at the sweatshop where she sewed furs with a taciturn Jewish couple and two talkative Irish ladies.

In those days it had been a rundown area, redolent in winter with the smell of coal fires and chips frying. Now it was residential, with clean pavements and the murmuring hush of a respectable middle-class street.

I took out the pocket electronic game I'd brought with me. I'd bought one for my son, and struck by some impulse to identify with him, I'd gone back and bought the same game for myself. Now I played desultorily with it. On the lighted face a small stick figure hurried up and down. A crocodile ran behind him, its jaws snapping open and shut. When I pressed the button, the little man jumped. He had an exhausted tortured look. I knew how he felt.

Around half past eleven a Mercedes drew up and five Indians, led by the Apache, got out. Goonay was a short, thin man with a greying beard and an intense look. I could imagine a big man like Winston being tempted to push him around, but from what I knew about him he didn't push willingly. His friends bulked round him, hiding his body from sight as they went up the stairs and entered the door.

I heaved a sigh of relief. Unless they'd already done the deal something should happen here. At least I seemed to be in the right place. But as soon as I had that thought it occurred to me that I might be wrong. If I was I'd have missed any chance of getting to Virginia and Roy and the action would happen somewhere else without me.

I banged the dashboard in frustration. Since all this had started I'd been following other people's activities. But it was like being in a savannah and knowing that something was moving about somewhere because you saw grasses bending. Everything was hidden except for these signs.

I was so taken up with my own mood that I only noticed Winston's car when it had gone past me. He parked some distance down the road on my side, and I slumped down so as not to be seen. Instead of getting out he switched off the lights and stayed there. I was peering through the windscreen trying to catch a glimpse of him, when another car drove slowly by. It was a red Golf. It stopped a little way past Winston's car and Roy got out and walked back. Winston got out in his turn and the two men stood on the pavement talking.

Under the street lights I could see Roy clearly. I recognised him from the photos, but he looked taller and stronger than I'd expected.

It was a look I'd seen before. Some young black men spent their time in prison body-building. The discipline, the relentless physical exercise and a limited diet gave them a distinctively healthy, muscled air. Roy also had his hair cut close to his scalp, and it made him look bullet-headed and powerful. As he and Winston walked up to the Apache's door, they seemed a formidable, unstoppable pair.

They went in and I wondered where Virginia was. Roy was driving her car so she was probably waiting somewhere. There was no point in worrying about it, I thought, if I could stay with Roy I'd get to her eventually.

They didn't stay long. After about fifteen minutes, just as I was running up a record score on my electronic game, they emerged with one of the Indians, walked across the road and got into Winston's car.

I pulled out behind them, my heart thumping with excitement. The Indian was sure to be taking them to a meeting, but I wasn't certain what I'd be doing there apart from keeping in touch with Roy. On the other hand, I'd have a better grip on the situation if I knew more about what was going on.

They pulled out into Green Lanes, a long road with only a slight curve, and I could see the red rear lights speeding towards Manor House from a long way off.

They kept straight on past the old Harringay Stadium, and turned left at Turnpike Lane. For a moment I expected them to stop at the house that Winston had visited previously, but they went straight past the turning and up towards Alexandra Palace. There was very little traffic on the road now and I dropped back to leave as much distance between us as possible.

I followed them through the archway that led to the palace, and from the foot of the hill I saw the red lights turn off into the yard that ran round the back of the building. I drove past, parked down the road on the other side, then got out and ran across the grass, back up the slope.

All the way up I was cursing myself for being a fool, but having come this far, I had to see what was happening. I reached the line of trees around the hill and ran crouching from one to the other, trying to control my breathing. I didn't know where they were and I peered through the darkness as I went.

About fifty yards from the top there was a cleared space, part of the artificial ski run that came down from below the gravelled surface of the yard. I paused there, and after a while I could see the outline of the car parked just off the grass, blending with the skips and builder's rubble scattered around.

I circled round towards the road so that I could get closer from behind the car, and I had crept to within a dozen yards when I heard another engine slowing into the turn.

I dropped flat into the long grass and a pair of headlights swept over my head. When I looked up again I saw a transit van standing just behind Winston's car.

The engine went out and I heard a door slam and footsteps crunching across the gravel. It was too dark to make out the faces, but I could see someone walking forward from the van.

They talked for a few minutes, but I was too far away to hear what was being said. As I strained to listen, the footsteps started crunching back in my direction.

At the same moment someone in the van shouted, a high, alarmed sound, and the others joined in with a chorus of yells.

The engine started up, racing, and almost immediately Winston's car whined and roared. The headlights went on, suddenly, and the blasted landscape of heaped concrete and rusty metal, which littered the yard, exploded into fragments of light and shade.

After the quiet and darkness, it was like being bombed with fireworks. I squirmed backwards and flattened myself against the ground, then nearly stood up in shock as a siren began to blast out close by.

Working it out slowly I realised that a police car must have crept up the hill then put its lights and siren on as it turned into the yard. Now it was sliding fast up the incline from the road.

The van was turning with a splash of gravel, and as the police car came up, roared straight at it.

Just before they collided the police car jinked right towards the grass and the van hit it a glancing blow on its side. It slewed sharply and whooshed past me on two wheels, then settled heavily lower down on the slope.

The engine stopped, and, when I looked, the other two vehicles were already turning into the road, their engines whining and screaming as they accelerated into the turn.

That was enough for me. I got moving from a sprinter's crouch and ran for my own car, going for the trees and making a wide detour round the police car. I was halfway down the slope when I heard the footsteps crashing behind me.

I veered to the right to try and get in a straight line to the car, but then I heard another set of footsteps running parallel, and I switched direction. In the confusion I must have lost my footing or stumbled because I was suddenly on the ground, gasping for breath. I was just getting up when a heavy body fell on me, knocking the wind out of my lungs again.

I lay still and two pairs of rough hands hauled me to my feet.

'Cunt,' a voice said in my ear. 'You're nicked.'

I gasped and spluttered while they pulled me back to the police car, my right arm shoved far up behind my back. I didn't want them to think I was totally undamaged, just in case they thought I might be getting off too lightly.

By now the air was full of police sirens, and by the time we arrived back at the wrecked vehicle, still flashing its blue light, another car was drawing up, followed by a van, out of which poured what seemed like a dozen policemen.

They handcuffed me quickly, but now it was all over and the spot was swarming with policemen, the atmosphere seemed more relaxed. I deduced that they hadn't caught Winston and his friends because there were so many of them standing round. My two captors stood close beside me. One of them was in plain clothes, the other was a uniformed man.

'All right,' the detective said. 'What's your name and what's going on here?'

I told him my name.

'I was taking a walk,' I said, 'when all this started happening.'

He laughed sarcastically.

'That's bleeding likely,' he said. 'Pull the other one.'

'Save your breath,' one of the policemen who'd just arrived said. 'Borelli wants him back at the station. Now.'

'Okay.'

The detective spun round and began pushing me towards the other car.

'What's the charge?' I said loudly.

'Fucking get in the car,' the detective said.

'Wait a minute,' a calmer voice said. It was an older uniform with sergeant's stripes.

'When we decide on the charge we'll let you know. Meantime sir, you're helping us with our enquiries. You'll be allowed to make a phone call at the station after you've seen the detective sergeant, if it's necessary.'

'Thank you.'

I got into the back seat of the car, and the detective got in beside me. We were there in five minutes or so, and they marched me rapidly up the steps to the desk. They took the handcuffs off, and the sergeant on duty looked bored as he told me to turn out my pockets. The detective hovered as if trying to emphasise that he had made an important catch.

Just as I had finished turning out my pockets, a man came up

102

behind me and, grabbing me roughly, rolled up the sleeves of my sweater and began looking at my arms.

'You're in trouble, mate,' he grunted while he did this. 'Are you a junkie or are you pushing? You might as well tell me now as later.'

I was facing him now, and I pursed my lips and shook my head. He had a low forehead with straw coloured hair falling over it, his close-set brown eyes peering through, and he was well above six feet, taller than me, with broad hulking shoulders.

'Leave off, Borelli,' I said, 'or at least say "please".'

'Detective Sergeant Borelli,' he snapped, his head jerking up to give me a brief glare. 'Mr Borelli to you, Sambo.'

'Sergeant,' the desk sergeant said. 'Look at this.'

His voice had a warning note, and I realised that he had found my NUJ card and was showing it to Borelli.

'A journalist?' Borelli said, and letting go of me took the card. Then he looked up, recognition dawning on his face.

'Sam?' he asked. 'Sam Dean?'

'Yes,' I told him, 'and if you don't stop feeling me up I'll bash your face in again.'

'Gordon Bennett.' He laughed and shook his head. 'I heard you'd become a reporter. What's all this then?'

'Well,' I hesitated. 'Can I talk to you now?'

'Yes.'

He nodded at the sergeant. 'I'll talk to him in the interview room. Come on, Sam.'

He turned and led the way, and I followed him, giving the detective, whose face was a picture of bewilderment, a little smile as I did so.

The smile was as much for myself as for him. I had last seen Borelli at school, and if anyone had told me then that one day I'd be glad to see him, I'd have laughed at the idea. Now we were greeting each other as if we'd been chums, but I'd fought Borelli twice in the first year and after that we'd hardly spoken to each other.

He'd been one of the playground bullies who sneered and jibed at vulnerable kids, and he'd left early with a few lame O-levels. The funny thing was that now, seeing him, I felt a kind of nostalgic warmth.

The little room we went into was furnished with a table and two chairs. He sat in one of them and gestured at the other. 'What's all this then?'

I rehearsed the story I'd been working out in the car.

'I'm working on a story about drugs, and a man rang me today and said there'd be a deal going down at Ally Pally. So I went for a look.'

'Is that all?'

'What else?'

'Why didn't you ring the police?'

'Come off it, Borelli. You can't do that every time some twit rings you with a bit of news. That happens several times a week, man. If it's convincing you check it out. I wasn't even all that convinced about this one. I just came for a look.'

'Who were you working for?'

I named a friend who ran a small news agency in South London. He would back me up, especially if it sounded as if there was a story in it.

Borelli nodded.

'I got the same tip, but I didn't take it all that seriously. Sounded like some Asian wally.'

'That's right,' I said.

'Why did you resist arrest?'

'I bloody didn't. It's dangerous creeping around pushers, you know. All hell broke loose so I ran. Next thing I know your morons are knocking me about.'

'Don't call them morons, Sam,' he said seriously. 'We can still get you on resisting arrest and failing to report knowledge of a crime.'

'What crime?'

'We'll find out,' he said. 'And if you're messing me about.'

He stopped and pointed a threatening finger.

'And I'd like to see you go into court with an innocent black reporter who your blokes duffed up after they missed the real villains.'

He sighed, got up and went out without speaking. In a moment he came back and held the door open.

'Okay Sam, you can piss off.'

I collected my belongings from the desk sergeant, whose bored expression hadn't changed.

'Here, Borelli,' I said on the way out. 'Ever see any of the others?'

'I nicked Bobby Owen a couple of years ago,' he said. 'Cannabis.'

'How could you do that to an old schoolmate, Borelli?'

'I enjoyed it,' he said. 'I always hated his guts.'

I shook my head and went out the door.

All this had taken less than an hour and I hailed a taxi so that I could go collect the car.

As I drove past the palace I could see a little group of policemen gathered around a breakdown truck was hauling their car off the slope. The lights flashed blue and yellow in the darkness, and I kept my speed carefully down to the twenty-five miles per hour speed limit.

The last thing I wanted was to be pulled again. Events were moving fast, and I had the feeling that I had no time to waste.

Chapter 19

I drove straight back towards Islington. The evening had yielded nothing except the knowledge that Winston and Roy's deal had somehow been screwed up, but apart from that I was none the wiser. I didn't know how to find Roy, and all I could hope was that I'd be able to pick up his trail at Goonay's. They'd probably have gone back there, and I might be able to follow Roy home.

I kept my fingers crossed all the way but it was one of those nights when everything seemed to go wrong, and as I swung in from Green Lanes, I saw immediately that both Winston's car and the red Golf had gone. I swore aloud as I parked. There was only one thing to do, and I got out of the car and hurried across the road before I could change my mind.

I gave the bell a long ring and the door opened before I could take my finger off it. It was the biggest of the Indians I'd seen with Goonay who answered, and he stood squarely in the doorway facing me. He wasn't so big, I thought, only an inch or two taller than me, but he had reddish glaring eyes which made him look tough and mean and a little bit crazy.

We stared at each other in silence for a few seconds.

'What do you want?' he said at last.

He sounded like a Brummie.

'I want to see Goonay.'

'He's not in.'

He stepped back quickly and slammed the door, too fast for me to stick my foot in it.

I stared at it for a little while, then put my finger on the bell again.

The door took longer to be opened this time. The same man was back, but he was now flanked by two equally tough-looking Indians.

'Fuck off or I'll smash you.'

Definitely a Brummie.

'Tell him Samson Dean wants to see him.'

'He doesn't want to see you.'

I'd had enough of this. I stepped back a little and spoke as loudly as I could.

'Goonay. I was at Ally Pally. Ally Pally. I want to talk to you.'

The red-eyed one stepped forward threateningly, and I braced myself. Just then a voice called out from the hallway behind them.

'Let him in. Let him in.'

They stood back a little, still glaring at me, and I pushed forward past them.

'Sorry fellas,' I said, smiling at them. 'Not this time.'

Goonay was standing at the end of the hallway with his hand stretched out to an open door. He was a short thin man with a beard and a luxuriant head of hair, both going grey.

'Samson Dean,' he said. 'It's a long time since we spoke.'

He had the posh accent of an anglicised Tamil, and it was even posher than when I first knew him. His hair had been black then, and he hadn't yet become a big-time fixer. I remembered lending him three pounds fifty, in front of Notting Hill tube station, more than ten years before, when he had been lean and broke. I hoped that he remembered it too.

We went into the sitting room and the rest of the men filed in behind him. The furniture was smart and comfortable in a chintzy way. I sat opposite Goonay in one of the armchairs.

'You're looking well,' he said. 'But you've put on a little weight.'

The wall behind him was lined with books. Goonay had always been interested in books and films and it looked as if he was still that way inclined.

I nodded. 'That's what happens.'

He smiled, raising his eyebrows and glancing sideways at one of his henchmen.

He looked back at me and the smile left his face.

'It's a bit late for a visit, Samson.'

'I came because I thought you might be able to help me.'

He spread his hands in a helpless gesture. 'How can I help you?'

'I'm looking for an address. I want to know how to get hold of Roy, the guy who hangs out with Winston, the big one.'

'I don't know those people,' Goonay said.

'They came here tonight,' I said. 'Then they went to Alexandra Palace with one of your people here.'

Somebody moved on my right, and Goonay said something sharp that I couldn't understand.

'What has that got to do with me?'

'I don't know. All I want is to find the guy.'

'I can't help you.'

'Goonay. I know about these things because you told the Boss and you must have known, in the circumstances, that he would tell me.'

'The Boss has a big mouth.'

'You know that, Goonay,' I said. 'You know the Boss as well as I do, and you wouldn't have told him, unless you were trying to spread the news about the deal. You wanted me to know, man.'

Goonay shrugged.

'Whatever the truth of it is, I can't tell you anything more. All this stuff is just rumour, you know.'

'Rumours,' I said. 'It's funny how these rumours get started. I mean, Detective Sergeant Borelli at the Hornsey nick thinks that a man with an Indian accent rang up and grassed about what was happening at Ally Pally.'

He made a dismissive gesture and his mouth twisted with contempt.

'These policemen. They'll say anything that suits their purpose.'

'Goonay,' I said. 'I know Borelli. We went to the same school.'

He stared at me for a long moment, then his face relaxed and he laughed.

'Well that's of no interest to me, but I just remembered. I think I can tell you where to find the skinhead.'

He gave me an address near Maida Vale. I got up, and two of the others stood up at the same time.

I looked down at Goonay.

'I know it's absolutely nothing to do with you,' I said. 'But if you had to make a guess, what do you think will happen with that deal? Off the record.'

He paused, still staring at me.

'Possibly the people involved will wait for a few days. In any case they'll want all the money before they hand over anything.'

'What about the money that's already been paid?'

He smiled and crooked his head on one side.

'That's all gone you know. There's a lot of overheads in business.'

I nodded and continued on my way out.

'Don't come back, Samson,' he said as I reached the door.

'Don't worry,' I told him. 'I won't.'

I started the engine and sat still, considering. It was already three o'clock, and I wanted to go home and sleep, but if I left it till the next day to look for the address Goonay had given me they might be gone by the time I got there. In addition I had the sense that the situation was developing fast, and, if I hoped to intervene, it was better to do it sooner rather than later.

I drove through Camden Town and over Primrose Hill into St John's Wood, and then turned left just before the motorway flyover.

The address Goonay had given me was in a block of luxury flats at the end of a cul-de-sac between Little Venice and the motorway. A short drive led into a courtyard where cars were parked but the gate was blocked by a padlocked iron rail.

I parked in the street and walked through.

The red Golf was parked at the end of a row in the far corner of the yard. I stood looking at it, my heart speeding up and my breath coming faster.

In a moment I went back to my car and took out the stick I carried in the back. It was made of a hard African wood, topped by a heavy carving of an elephant. I had bought it in Kenya and I carried it now as a sort of lucky charm.

I hefted it, remembering the way Winston's fist had smashed into my stomach, and walked back to the lighted glass door at the entrance to the flats, but when I pushed it didn't open.

109

I hesitated. I didn't want to ring the number Goonay had given me, partly because I wouldn't know what to say if they answered, and I didn't want them to be ready for me.

I started ringing the bells at the top, and after I'd pressed the fourth one, a buzzer sounded. I pushed the door quickly and it opened.

I went on through, and up the stairs, moving cautiously, but no one looked out.

I didn't have to tiptoe because the stairs were thickly carpeted. My footsteps didn't make a sound.

The flat was on the second floor and I rang the bell wearily. Getting through doors was beginning to feel like a life's work.

I could see a gleam of light through the glass at the top of the door, but no one answered. I rang again, and kept on ringing for nearly a full minute, but there was still no answer.

I took my finger away and thought about the problem. Eventually I rang again, then bent down and shouted through the letter box, 'It's Oscar. Winston sent me.'

Suddenly I heard a scrabbling noise behind the door and it opened about an inch. Part of a woman's face peered through the crack and when the searching eye found me there was a movement and I sensed that she was about to slam it shut. I shoved my shoulder hard against the wood, and it sprang open with a crash, sending her flying into the wide hallway. I stepped in and slammed the door shut behind me as the girl, who I'd recognised as Virginia, yelled out for Roy.

He was already charging at me from a room beyond and to the right of the hall.

I don't know whether he saw the stick in my hand, but I was determined not to let him get close enough to grapple me with his big muscles. As he reached me I swayed left and whacked him just above the knees with the stick.

He fell forward past me against the door, and I turned fast and hit him as hard as I could, front and side, just below the ribs. He went down, slumped on the carpet in front of the door.

But he wasn't out. He clutched his stomach and struggled to rise, so I held the point of the stick over him, only a few inches away from his eyes.

'Don't move,' I shouted above the noise of Virginia screaming. She hadn't moved in the few seconds the little battle had taken, but now she got her reflexes together to make a rush at me. I held out my left arm in a stiff gesture, the fingers pointing at her, and she stopped in her tracks.

'I'm not the police,' I said quickly. 'I'm not going to hurt you. I just want to talk.'

She looked uncomprehending.

'Your parents sent me,' I said loudly and emphatically. 'I just have to talk to you.'

Without replying she came past me, her shoulders slumped and her eyes downcast, and knelt beside Roy, feeling his stomach where he held on to it, and rubbing it.

'Do you understand?' I said. 'Is it all right? Can we talk? I've got things to tell you. I only want to talk.'

She nodded. Roy groaned.

'All right?' I repeated.

'Yes,' she said in a voice so quiet I could hardly hear it. 'It's all right.'

'Okay,' I said, leaning against the wall. I put the stick down and bent over to help Roy up, but he shook my hand off with a snarl.

'Who are you?' Virginia asked me, looking up.

I grinned.

In spite of everything I felt a sort of triumph. It was like coming to the end of a long road, and I had found them alive and well. It was easy to smile.

'I'm Samson Dean,' I told her.

Chapter 20

We sat in the big kitchen of the flat. There was enough room round the table to seat eight people, ten at a pinch.

'Nice place,' I said, looking around.

'I'm not going home,' Virginia said.

'I'm not bothered,' I told her. 'The thing is your parents were worried. They got this big ransom demand. I mean you know about that? It scared the shit out of them.'

'It's my money,' she said defensively.

She had a blank, serious face which could look arrogant in the way of women of her age and class who are quite sure that they're pretty. But she was extravagantly thin, so much so that her head seemed a little big for her body; and her blue eyes looked watery and wandering.

As if sensing what I was thinking she got up, went to a cupboard in the corner, opened a drawer and put on a pair of sunglasses.

'If it was your money right now you wouldn't have had to play that kind of trick to get your hands on it.'

'They got what was coming to them,' Roy said. His voice had the nasal sound of Lancashire. 'It's none of your business anyway.'

He was sitting upright now, but there was something about his eyes which put me in mind of a lonely and frightened little boy, and I felt sorry, for a moment, that I had hit him so hard.

'Don't talk balls,' I said. 'If the police had found you, you would be in big trouble right now. Well nicked. You know what I mean?'

His face lost some of the assurance that had been coming back to it.

'They wouldn't get the police,' Virginia said flatly.

'They called me,' I said. 'Why did you need the money anyway?'

'Living is expensive,' Roy smirked sarcastically and glanced at Virginia.

With the dark glasses on her expression was unreadable. She didn't smile.

'I know life is expensive,' I said, playing along with him, 'but most people don't need that much to get by.'

'Well now you've seen me,' Virginia said impatiently. 'What are you going to do? Are you supposed to run off and tell them where I am?'

I didn't answer. I didn't know quite what I wanted to do now that I was facing them across the table.

'I'll pay you,' she said. 'If you just leave us alone. I suppose they're paying you. I'll pay you more.'

'What about all this kidnap shit? I'm going to have to tell your parents you're not in any danger.'

'That's all over. All I need is some time without being hassled.'

'Everybody needs that. But you need another fifty grand on top.'

She was silent for a little while, staring at me. Opposite me Roy hunched over and stared at the table.

'What do you mean?' she said eventually. 'I only asked them for twenty.'

I looked at Roy. He looked away from me.

'Why don't you ask Roy? He knows.'

She looked at Roy. He smiled and stroked his head with one hand.

'What's going on?'

She didn't sound angry, but there was a sharp edge to her voice.

'I was going to tell you,' he said rapidly. 'If this get hadn't come bursting in. We had to pay out some more money, and we phoned them.'

'God,' Virginia put her face in her hands and moaned.

'We had to do it, otherwise the whole deal would have been fucked. We'd have lost the twenty with nothing to show for it.'

'You've got nothing to show now.'

'We're sorting it out, Virge. We'll have it sorted in a couple of days.'

I laughed. Virginia's mouth twisted in a hopeless gesture, and she looked back and forth between me and Roy.

'Sorting it out? Did he tell you what happened at Ally Pally? Never mind your big deal. I bet you don't even have a little stash.'

Virginia's mouth trembled and grimaced, and she pressed her right hand hard against it.

'What do you bleeding know about it?' Roy snarled.

For a moment it seemed that he was going to launch himself across the table at me, and I braced myself, but then Virginia leaned over and shouted at him.

'Fifty thousand? What's it for? I thought we agreed.'

His eyes flickered back to her and took on a hunted look. He settled back into his seat.

'Something happened. The customs seized some of it or something. I don't know. It's not like bloody going into a shop and buying twenty fags. They said it was another ten thousand. We had to have it.'

'He said fifty.'

'I didn't know Winston was going to say fifty. What's the difference anyway?'

'You fucking idiots,' Virginia hissed. 'It's different. You can't just put your hands on twenty thousand then follow it up by fifty thousand just like that. You can't do it. That kind of cash is hard to get. Don't you know that?'

She had a hysterical look behind the glasses. Since the first demand for money she'd had time to think about it, and I had a hunch she now regretted what was happening to her parents. It struck me that this was the first time since all this had started that she'd had to face what was really happening, and the effect her actions might be having on other people.

It was hard to believe, but I'd met kids like that before. What they wanted was right. Until they ran up against a bigger

114

reality, and if there was enough money around that might never happen. Sometimes only death could stop them.

Roy eyed her resentfully and she looked straight back at him, her eyes wide and steady behind the dark lenses. Even in those circumstances it was easy to see she was her mother's daughter.

Roy's eyes slid away from her. 'They can get it,' he said sullenly.

'What are you going to do then?' I asked him.

'What's it got to do with you?'

'I was at Alexandra Palace tonight.'

That got their attention. Now I had the initiative and I told them what I had seen at Ally Pally.

'They're not coming back for a while. Besides I bet you don't know if they're conning you, do you? Winston might be conning you, come to think of it, and you don't know bugger all.'

'Fuck off,' he growled, but he sounded uncertain.

'You think about it, Virginia,' I said. 'Dealing with a few ounces is one thing. But these people are different. If they feel like fiddling you, they will and they can and all. They've got connections. It's a business to them. They can just walk off and say screw you, or they can come round and give you a nice overdose.'

'No chance,' Roy said. 'No chance at all. Not us, chum.'

He laughed grimly, but Virginia didn't look reassured.

'He's full of shit,' I told Virginia. 'He's full of shit, you know.'

I was feeling a sort of light-headed impatience with this lot. It was like trying to talk a pair of miserable kids into wiping their noses.

'Do you know what happened to your friends?'

'Who? What are you on about?'

'Your friends Dick and Sally. Do you know what happened?'

'They've not been busted have they?' She sounded bored and indifferent.

'No. They haven't been busted. They're dead.'

What I could see of Virginia's face panicked.

'Dead? When did that happen? Did they have an accident?'

'If you think that those two having a double overdose is an accident. Yes. They had an accident.'

'Both of them? At the same time?' She sounded stunned.

'Your pal Winston was there. Didn't he tell you?'

'Winston?'

I nodded.

She leaned over and plucked at Roy.

'Did you know this?'

'No, I didn't and I don't believe it. I don't know what this geezer's after, but don't you see he's trying to wind us up? It's a wind-up.'

She looked back at me uncertainly. She didn't know what to believe now.

'Ring them up,' I said. 'See if they're there. If you'd been reading the local paper you'd have seen it.'

Without a word she got up and went into the hallway, and I heard her pick up the phone. Roy sat motionless, staring at the table.

'I went to see your Aunt Shirley. She said to tell you she was still there.'

He didn't look up.

'You want to mind your own fucking business.'

The words were angry but his heart wasn't in it. He was thinking furiously and he sounded more worried than anything else.

Virginia came back.

'They're not there.'

'They could be out,' Roy said.

'Not at this hour. Besides they hardly ever go out. They just wouldn't be out now. It must be true.'

I could think of other reasons why they mightn't answer but she was in a frame of mind to believe me.

'Of course it's true,' I said. 'I saw them just after Winston left the flat.'

I told them about waiting outside, and then going in and seeing the corpses. Talking about it in the early morning silence was eerie. When I told them how cold the couple's flesh had been Virginia shivered involuntarily.

'I think Winston gave them the stuff, and he sat and watched them go.'

'He wouldn't do that,' Roy said, but there was a shadow of something frightened in his voice.

'I don't know. He didn't exactly react like a man of peace when I tried to talk to him outside. I can still feel it where he bashed me. He was in a hurry.'

116

'What do you expect?'

Roy smiled as if the thought amused him. I knew he was trying to needle me, but even so his smirk was irritating.

'I expect you to tell me what's going on.'

'We don't have to tell you anything,' he said.

'No, you don't. I want to help you sort this out, but don't sit there thinking that you don't have to bother because the Bakers won't go to the cops, because I will. At the moment Dick and Sally look like an accidental overdose, but if I tell them about Winston being there, and about what's been going on, Ally Pally and everything, I reckon you'll both be very deep in shit by tomorrow morning. You can't afford it, man. Just think about it.'

'What do you want to know?' Virginia said suddenly.

'Just begin at the beginning.'

If either of them recognised that as the piece of literary corn it was they gave no sign.

Virginia said that Roy had approached her at the college. 'About a month ago. At first I thought he was just a weirdo, but then he told me some things and we started talking.'

'He told you he was your brother?'

'How do you know?' Virginia's eyebrows shot up with amazement. 'Did they tell you? Did they admit it?'

'No. They said that was what Roy said. How do you know it's true?'

Roy grunted derisively.

'I didn't believe it at first. But eventually I did. He's got a birthmark. A sort of triangle-shaped red mark, just here.' She pointed at her back, just above the buttocks. She laughed. 'He didn't even know about it until I told him. We've all got it. The mark of the Bakers.'

She laughed sarcastically. I glanced at Roy but his expression didn't change.

'After that we just hung out. Getting to know each other. I had a few rows with my parents about Roy.'

'Why?'

Behind the dark glasses I could just see her looking at him out of the corner of her eye.

'My father,' she corrected herself, '*our* father wouldn't admit that Roy was my brother. It was so mean. It made me so angry. I hated them. I really did.'

117

Now she sounded like a child.

'Is that why you agreed to blackmail them?'

'That was nothing to do with it. Not really. Roy had to have some money. We had to have capital for a deal.'

I smiled. Dealing was the most stable cottage industry among addicts, and all kinds of small-time wheeler-dealers were moving into the business. In the sixties people could make a regular living by dealing grass. Only now it was smack and coke, and the profits were bigger.

'Dick introduced us to this guy, and we fixed up a deal. It's my money but I knew they wouldn't give it to me. It was the only way we could get our hands on it.'

'What's Dick and Sally got to do with it? Why would anyone want to kill them?'

'They just introduced us to this guy. That's all. I don't know.'

'You know, don't you?' I said to Roy. 'Someone must have sent Winston round.'

Roy sighed impatiently. 'All right. All I know is the guy was trying it on. He went round to see some of those people we were dealing with and said he wanted a commission. They told him to piss off, but then they started coming down on me. They said they were going to do something about him if we didn't. They wanted Dick to get out of the way. Go down to the coast or something for a couple of weeks, till the action was over. A couple of junkies like them could talk to the wrong people. Any time.'

'So they got killed instead.'

'I don't know,' he said. 'They just had to be told, you know. I don't know what happened. It was likely a fucking accident.'

He shouted the last words at me. I didn't reply. There seemed to be nothing to say. Virginia too was silent, sitting bolt upright, twisting her fingers in and out of each other on the table top. Somewhere outside a car horn suddenly hooted and I listened for the sound of an engine. But there was nothing except the early morning silence.

'What are you going to do?' Virginia asked me.

'I'm going home to get some sleep. In the morning I'm going to phone your parents and tell them where you are and that you're not in any danger. All right?'

I watched Roy in case he was tempted to jump me, but he

118

didn't make a move. He looked tired and defeated, with a sad, hurt, look in his eyes. I guessed that at the beginning he had half expected things to go wrong in the end. Nothing had ever gone right for him.

'You don't need advice from me, but I think you ought to talk to your father again. Go and see him and just talk to him. Don't threaten or come on all tough. Just talk. Maybe this time he's ready to listen.'

Roy didn't move and I looked at Virginia. She had her chin resting on one hand, covering her mouth.

'Don't use him to attack your parents,' I said. 'It's not fair. Maybe if you help they can work something out.'

When I played all that back to myself it sounded like somebody's uncle talking, and I certainly wasn't any relative of hers so I shut up.

'I can't go home again,' she said. 'Not now. Not like this.'

'Yes, you can,' I told her. 'There's nowhere else. If you want to help Roy, pack this in. He can't handle it and neither can you. I don't think this deal is going to happen any more, and all the other things are happening round you because you can't control them and you can't stop them happening. And it's all because you started it. You know that. The best thing now is to run and hide while you can.'

Neither of them replied, so I pushed myself back from the table and struggled to my feet. With only a very little encouragement I could have got down on the floor and gone to sleep.

Perhaps it was the fatigue I was feeling, but I could think of nothing more to say. I turned and walked to the door. With my hand on the door handle I looked back at them. They were still sitting as if frozen, in the same position.

'Goodnight folks,' I said.

Chapter 21

When I woke up I couldn't remember any dreams. I remembered Roy and Virginia and their bad luck expressions, though. I wondered vaguely what they were doing, and at that moment the phone rang. For a little while I lay there counting the rings and telling myself that I would get out of bed the next instant and answer it, but I was feeling agreeably paralysed, and somehow I couldn't move. After I'd counted about twenty the ringing stopped, and I laughed a little with relief.

I was done with all that. The runaways had been found. What they did from now on was up to them. I hadn't told the Bakers but they'd probably know by now, and that could wait.

I got up, drank a cup of coffee and rang Sophie. She wasn't in but her answerphone told me to leave a message. I told it my name and said I'd like to see her later on. Then I went out and strolled slowly down Edgware Road.

It was a fresh, bright day. The sun peeped out from behind the grey fluff in the sky and eyed the street suspiciously. I smiled back to show that everything was cool, and it hovered for a while, but then I turned in to a newsagent's shop and it ducked out of sight.

It was past noon and I bought the evening paper. The front page announced another rape murder and I put it under my arm. I didn't want to read it.

After another few minutes' walking I turned off, threaded my way through the market and approached the barbershop.

It was a real barbershop, not a hairdresser's or a salon.

Two West Indian barbers stood behind the chairs clipping hair and chatting with the customers – three or four of them, who sat waiting on the cracked red leather benches which lined the walls. The barbers waved their scissors at me, and I sat down with a distinct sense of pleasure.

Being in this place was like a kind of reward. As a child I had visited a barbershop like this with my father nearly every fortnight. One of my favourite memories was of perching next to him, silent while he talked and joked with the barbers.

Sitting there I had the uncanny feeling that at any moment he might walk in through the door. 'Cut it right down,' he'd say, looking sternly at me. 'Cut it clean.'

'Pity about that fella Bruno fought a while back. Heard about that?'

The barber holding the floor was tall, with long sideburns and a lugubrious expression. A Grenadian, I thought.

'What happened?' the shorter barber asked.

The Grenadian beamed and winked at me.

'He got stabbed the other night, didn't you hear? They had it on the news. What's his name?'

'Witherspoon?'

'No,' the Grenadian said. 'It was with a knife.'

He laughed, stepping back from the customer in the chair to give himself room. I'd heard it before, but I laughed along with everyone else. It was a nice, companionable feeling.

I opened the paper, avoiding the front page, and let the talk wash over me. Back home thirty years ago and thousands of miles away, the shop might have been smaller and dirtier, the barbers less well dressed, but essentially it was the same. I sat back drowsy and secure. I felt like going to sleep all over again. Perhaps I'd dream about my dad.

In the end I didn't go to sleep, but, walking home, I felt as rested and relaxed as if I had. The only prickle of discomfort came from the cold feeling around my ears and the back of my neck. Under the surface of well-being I kept getting flashes of naked vulnerability.

I suppressed them. This was an afternoon for mooching around and taking it easy, I thought. I changed my mind as soon as I got to the top of the stairs, because I could hear the phone ringing.

It sounded as if it had no intention of stopping until I answered, and even before I picked it up I knew that trouble was on the way.

It was Tess Baker, and she sounded as if she was barely holding hysteria in check.

'Virginia,' she said. 'That man rang again.'

'What?'

I couldn't make sense of it for a moment. All that was over.

'A man rang up,' she said. 'He said she wasn't coming home. I've been trying to ring you.'

I told her I'd be there in fifteen minutes and put the phone down. On my way over I was cursing myself for being careless. It didn't take too much imagination to figure out what had happened. While I was sleeping in and mooching around Winston had turned up and persuaded or forced them to change their plans. Now it all had to be done again.

And perhaps, I thought, my heart leaping with panic, they might be in real trouble this time.

The traffic wasn't heavy and I got there in about twenty minutes. Tess opened the door immediately, as if she'd been standing behind it. She turned away without a word and led me into the big room overlooking the garden.

The phone call had come a couple of hours ago. It was a man with a deep voice. She's not coming home, he'd said. Then he asked her whether she'd got the money yet. Fifty thousand pounds or they'd never see her again. Tess made a faint choking sound and pressed her fist against her mouth as she told me.

'I asked him for proof,' she said. 'He put her on and she said to do what he wanted. She sounded terrified. Then he came on again and said he wanted the money in cash by tonight. I said we couldn't do it so soon and he said tomorrow. I tried to argue with him but he wouldn't listen. He said that if we called the police he would do things to her. Terrible things. And even if they found them he could prove she had financed buying and selling drugs. It was her money. He said if he went down she'd go with him. He said he'd finish us all, starting with her.' Towards the end of her story she was shuddering and gasping like an accident victim.

'Okay,' I said soothingly. I didn't feel very calm myself, but if I wasn't careful we'd both be screaming and climbing the walls. 'Take it easy. At least he won't hurt her and we've got time to sort it out.'

I put my arm round her shoulder and patted her. She leaned against me for an instant and I felt her trembling. Suddenly she jerked herself upright.

'You don't understand,' she said. 'He said he was giving her heroin. He said he'd give it to her every day, as much as she wants, as much as she could take. He said we'd be responsible for what happened.'

'Did you tell your husband all this?'

'I haven't spoken to him. Pete's trying to reach him.'

Her voice rose to a shrill, high sound. Her face was red and swollen, and her eyes glared. As if she knew what I was thinking she turned her face away, and I put my arm round her again. She rested her weight on me, and her breasts heaved against my chest. It struck me that if the circumstances had been different I'd have been turned on. Even as it was, the heat of her body was affecting me.

Struggling against the mood I got up abruptly. In the next moment I remembered Roy.

'Did she ring you before?'

'No.'

I took a deep breath and told her what had happened the previous night and that they had meant to turn up that morning.

'Why didn't you tell us?' Her voice was shrill again, and angry.

'I'm telling you now. And anyway I thought the best thing was to let it happen. You've got a lot to sort out yourselves. That's not my business.'

She made another noise that sounded angry.

'I'm going to the flat where I saw them,' I said. 'I'll ring you from there.'

At the door I looked round. She hadn't moved.

'It'll be all right,' I said.

She didn't move or give any sign that she'd heard me. Perhaps she wasn't convinced. I wasn't convinced myself.

123

Chapter 22

There were fewer cars in front of the block of flats in Maida Vale, but otherwise it looked the same. I went across to the door and started ringing the bells from the top. Suddenly a metallic voice spoke.

'Who is it?'

I leaned close to the grille and whispered, 'It's me.'

The buzzer sounded and I pushed the door open, and ran for the second floor. In front of the flat I pressed the bell. One long ring. Nothing happened. Up above me a door opened and after a while slammed shut again. I peered through the letter box but I could only see darkness behind it. I pressed the bell again. Nothing.

In a minute I made up my mind. This was a private block where most people would probably be out at work. I moved back a little and smashed my heel against the door. It seemed to make a lot of noise. The door shifted a little but didn't open. I tried it again, and, third time lucky, it sprang open and smashed against the wall. I went in quickly, and closed the door behind me.

The kitchen door was closed and I turned the knob and pushed it, but there was something behind it that stopped it from opening.

I pushed hard and it yielded slowly. When the gap was big enough for me to squeeze through I stuck my head into it and looked down. Roy was lying against the door, his body bent and twisted.

124

My heart turned over. This was my fault.

I almost backed away before I realised that he was moving. I squeezed through the doorway and took a closer look. His body had seemed twisted because his hands and feet were tied together behind his back. There was a broad band of elastoplast stuck across his mouth. He looked unhurt apart from a swelling and a bruise on his face. I hadn't given him that. He grunted desperately and looked around till I found a knife by the sink and cut him loose.

I helped him up and let him undo the tape himself. As I expected, his first words were a burst of furious obscenities.

'What happened?' I asked him.

'Fuck off,' he said.

He sat down at the table and leaned on his elbows, his shoulders hunched over. I sat opposite him.

'What are we going to do now?'

He didn't reply.

'Let's put it another way,' I said. 'What are you going to do now?'

Still no answer. He didn't even shift his position.

'We have to do something,' I said. 'At least you could tell me what went on. If the fact that she's your sister doesn't bother you, imagine what happens to you if she's dead or injured. You know what I mean?'

That brought some reaction. He looked at me then looked away again.

'Give me a clue,' I said.

'He came this morning,' he said. 'We told him we were packing it in. Virginia said she'd give him some money. He said okay. The bastard cracked on like he didn't mind. We thought it was all right. Then he went down the car to get some grass, and came back with a shotgun. He hit me.'

He paused and shook his head as if he couldn't believe it.

'Bastard hit me. Then he tied me up and telephoned Virginia's mum.'

'What did you expect?'

I thought he was going to swear at me again, but he merely shrugged.

'Did he say where he was going?'

He shook his head.

'Do you know where he might go?'

He shook his head again.

'Come on,' I said. 'He's your mate. You must know something.'

'He's got a cousin in Paddington.'

'Where does he live?'

'I don't know.'

This wasn't going anywhere. I got up and rang the Bakers. I got Baker. He'd rushed back home, he said, as soon as he'd spoken to Tess.

'What are you going to do?' I asked him.

'I don't know.'

This was getting repetitive.

'Can you pay the money?'

'Not tomorrow.'

'You can't?'

'I might be able to if I had a lot of time.' He paused. 'It's a lot of money. That wouldn't matter so much but you just can't walk into a bank and say give me fifty thousand pounds.'

'Okay, but maybe you should try and think of something. Probably your best bet is to get the cops.'

'No,' he said sharply. 'It's not that simple.'

We were both silent for a while.

'What about Roy?' I asked him.

'Roy?'

I told him briefly what had happened to Roy.

'I think he might help.'

There was another short pause, as if he was thinking about it.

'I think I'd like to see him,' he said in a quiet, subdued voice.

'I'll bring him over,' I told him.

I put the phone down and looked back at Roy. He was still sitting hunched over at the table.

'Are you stopping here?'

He shook his head.

'No. This place belongs to a cousin or something of Virginia's.'

'Where will you go?'

'I don't know.'

He shrugged as if he didn't care where he went, and I supposed that he didn't. All his schemes had fallen apart, and there was nothing left.

126

'We'd better go and see your father,' I said. 'I think we ought to sort out something about Virginia. Otherwise it will hang over you and God knows what will happen.'

He looked at me as if he was going to say something angry and dismissive. Then he changed his mind and looked back at the table.

'You coming?'

He didn't answer for a long moment, then he seemed to make up his mind.

'All right. I'm coming.'

Chapter 23

I drove back to my flat. I wasn't ready yet for the Bakers, and Roy didn't seem to be in too much of a hurry. When I told him we'd get there in a couple of hours he simply nodded. On the way I looked at him out of the corner of my eye. He stared straight ahead.

This was my chance to talk to him, but I didn't know how to begin. I looked sideways again, but his position hadn't changed. Maybe he was going to give me the silent treatment.

I shrugged. When I was his age I thought all people above a certain age were peculiar. A middle-aged man who got me in his car and tried to pry into my inner life would probably be the strangest of all.

I laughed out loud at that, and he looked sideways at me. That's right boy, I thought. I'm a weirdo.

But he surprised me.

'How's my auntie?' he asked.

'What?'

'My auntie. You said you saw her.'

'She's fine. She's really worried about you.'

'Yeah.' He laughed softly. 'She's something else, you know. One time we had a leak in the ceiling. It kept coming all wet down the wall. They wouldn't come and do it. You know how they are.'

I knew. I'd spent over a year there tramping back and forth with tenants' complaints.

'She went down the Housing one morning. I was holding on to her hand. She squeezed me so hard it hurt. I kept telling her, leave go auntie. Well we got there and the geezer started messing her about, and suddenly she just got up and started screaming. They couldn't stop her. Eventually they got her in the manager's office and calmed her down with a cup of tea. Then she got up and told them she was coming back every day. Twice a day. Twice. You should have seen their fucking faces. Twice a day. Next day they were fixing the leaks. They never messed with her again.'

Great. These were his memories. I wondered how many hours he'd spent down the Social, the Housing, the clinic, holding on to auntie's hand. I nodded.

'You're right. She's something else.'

He looked at me, smiling a little.

'I used to see you,' he said.

'Me?'

'Yeah. You used to hang out with Mr Heywood.'

I thought a little. Heywood used to teach at a school near Moss Lane.

'You used to go to a pub in Princess Road. Then you used to go down the flats.'

This guy could have made up a file on my movements. I smiled back at him, imagining him as a wide-eyed boy. He'd have had longer, curly hair then, probably with little reddish streaks proclaiming his origins.

'I haven't seen Heywood for years,' I said.

'He used to take us for football.'

He loved football, he told me. He had been in the school team, and it was the only thing that kept him going, until he got into trouble, then it was all over. His face lost its animation.

'Is that where you met Winston?'

He shook his head.

'No. Winston was at Risley.'

'The remand centre?'

'Yeah. Risley.'

Risley was where they educated black boys like Roy. Since then he'd been a good graduate, pointed shotguns at people, broken his auntie's heart and done time.

I ushered him up the stairs of the flat and showed him into my

129

tiny sitting room, then went to make some coffee. When I came
back he was looking at my books. He picked up one of them as I
came in, and read the title slowly. *The Psychological Consequences
of Being a Black American.*

'What's that all about then?' he said.

'It's about what happens to your head, people like you and
me, when pressure hits.'

He looked at me curiously. 'You're really into all this.'

'What?'

'Racism and all that.'

'I'm interested in what makes me tick. Aren't you?'

'Yes.' He hesitated, uncertain. These were deep waters. 'I
used to go to these black history classes inside. It was all like,
solidarity. Some of them guys were really into it.'

I nodded. I was about to ask him more about it when he put
the book down abruptly and pointed at the TV.

'Can I put it on?'

'Yes.'

It was news time. There'd been a bomb blast somewhere in
the Middle East. We'd missed the opening introduction but the
camera was panning slowly along a line of stretchers. Later on
there was a series of pictures of heavily bandaged children.

'What about these drugs then?'

'What drugs?'

He sounded snappish.

'Virginia was using something,' I said.

'That wasn't me. She was into that before I ever saw her. I
never touched it.'

'What about Winston?'

'Come on. We used to train together down the gym.'

'But you were dealing.'

'That was different. It was just the money. It was Virginia's
idea. We were just dealing a bit of grass you know. Nothing
heavy. Then we started talking about doing a big one.'

Virginia's friends had the contacts, he told me. They were
out to make a big score. Winston was going to take his cut and
set up some kind of business in the Midlands.

'What about you?'

'Africa. I was going to Africa.' He looked straight at me.
Defiant.

'What were you going to do there?'

'I don't know. Spend some time. See some places. Get to know people. Work somewhere.'

It sounded crazy, but it was a black dream we all had at some time or the other. Sometimes I caught myself thinking that if I didn't make the trip now it would soon be too late.

'What about your father?'

He didn't answer at first, and the silence between us seemed to stretch out interminably. Then, suddenly, he began to talk.

'I used to make up stories about him,' he said. 'When I was little I told the other kids he was in the States. I said he was an athlete, then I said he was a musician.'

I looked at him. I had meant to ask about the ransom, but now he was in a world of his own, talking about something different.

'I dreamed about him all the time.'

In prison he dreamed that his father had come and opened the doors and they'd walked out together. Later on, when he'd found out who his father actually was, the hardest thing to bear was that Baker had known about him all along. He had been full of rage.

Listening to him was touching and embarrassing. His voice was so full of emotions which were naked and deep. I broke in and asked him a question to stop him, move him on to something else.

'What about Winston? What's his part in all this?'

'He's my mate.' Then he remembered and corrected himself. 'He was.'

He told me the rest quickly. Winston had been brought up in care. He had nowhere to go. He was big and he was good with his fists. That was all.

'Do you think he'll do anything to her?'

'I don't know. Depends on what's happening. He goes mad if people mess him about.'

'How come you picked up with a guy like him?'

'You don't understand. When you make friends inside it's real. It has to be. He's my mate.'

He was wrong about my not understanding. I did. There was a ridiculously large number of young black men in prison, and black men in a white man's prison needed each other. The ex-prisoners I knew always talked about the way they had become brothers inside.

When Winston and Roy fell out it must have been a trauma, and perhaps that feeling had gone both ways.

Whatever it was they'd felt, they would probably now be unforgiving to each other. When brothers fall out, they do it without mercy or tolerance.

Chapter 24

As we approached the Bakers' house I could feel Roy's reluctance and confusion. To try and ease the tension I began telling him about the days when I had first arrived in Britain as a child.

Nowadays, I told him, it was hard to imagine living anywhere except London.

He looked at me with his eyebrows raised and I amended that. There were a number of places where I'd fancy living but that wasn't what I meant.

'Do you think he wants to see me?' Roy asked. We were just pulling into the kerb in front of the Bakers' house.

'Yes,' I said firmly and without hesitation. 'Of course.'

Tess answered the door. She turned without speaking and led the way back into the room overlooking the garden. Baker was standing there and he stretched his hand out to Roy.

He looked pale, but his blue eyes had sharpened to a glittering fixity. Tess walked past him, and sat down facing the window. She hadn't spoken to Roy, but when her eyes rested on him her expression was contemptuous, almost disgusted.

Roy and Baker shook hands. I had the sense that Baker wanted to embrace Roy, but it wasn't something he could do.

'I'll take Roy into the study for a talk.'

He said this to his wife's profile. She gave a tight, small smile. His eyes flicked over me without apparent recognition as he turned away and took Roy's elbow.

Watching them go through the door I noticed how much alike they were. At first glance the colour and the hair made them seem different, but a closer look revealed that they were the same height, and they held their shoulders at the same square angle.

When the door closed I went over and sat opposite Tess. She looked at me without expression.

'We haven't had our instructions yet,' she said in a flat, dead voice. 'I'm expecting the phone to ring any minute.'

I cast around for something reassuring.

'I don't think he'll hurt her.'

She didn't reply. There was nothing more to say and Tess didn't seem to be in the mood for small talk, so we sat in silence looking out at the garden.

When the phone rang it split the silence like a sudden shriek. Tess got up and answered it before I could move or say anything. Watching her I saw her shoulders droop and her position relax. It wasn't Winston. She told the person on the other end that she was waiting for a call and she'd ring them back. Then she replaced the receiver quietly and sat down again.

In the moment when she'd answered, though, I'd had an idea. Somehow I hadn't been thinking till then. If we arranged a handover we'd need some kind of plan to make sure that Winston didn't do a fiddle. I guessed that he would take whatever price he could get as long as it wasn't ridiculously low, and he'd fix some inaccessible spot for the swap.

Our insurance would be to wait on the spot in case anything went wrong. Unless he had help he wouldn't spot us, and if we could choose the place we'd have a real advantage. I asked Tess whether they had the use of a place outside of London. Somewhere quiet and isolated.

She nodded. Yes. A house in Buckinghamshire. About an hour and a half out of London.

'When he rings,' I told her, 'get him to take her there.'

She frowned at me, and I explained.

'Won't he already have something in mind?'

'He doesn't know London all that well, and if he's got somewhere in mind you can convince him that it may be dangerous. Tell him you might be followed. In your position it might stir up a lot of curiosity if you're prancing around with all that money in a suitcase.'

'It won't be all that money.'

I shrugged, and she considered me carefully.

'Won't he suspect something?'

'He'll suspect something in any case. Persuade him.'

She seemed to be about to say something else, but just then the door opened and her husband came in, followed by Roy. The atmosphere between them had changed. Roy still looked sullen, but the tension had gone and Baker seemed almost relaxed.

'Any word?' he asked.

Tess shook her head. 'Nothing yet.'

He looked at me.

'It will take time to raise that kind of sum.'

'I'd try and get it over as quickly as you can,' I told him. 'Offer him what you can raise tomorrow. I shouldn't think he'd want to drag the whole thing out either. Perhaps it would be easier for him up North, but down here his resources will be limited. He'll probably give you a bargain.'

Baker nodded thoughtfully and the phone rang.

Tess picked it up and listened without speaking.

'Is my daughter there?' she said suddenly. 'Is she? Let me speak to her.'

Virginia must have come on because in a moment Tess asked her if she was all right. Her voice cracked with anxiety and fear.

Baker got up and I waved him back. He sat down without protest.

'We haven't got that much,' Tess said. She paused. 'Ten thousand.'

A few seconds passed while she listened, and she took a couple of deep breaths, pulling herself together.

'I don't care what you do. It would take a couple of weeks at least. We could manage ten thousand tomorrow, but that is it. It's up to you.'

Her face was white and she was clutching convulsively at the table, but she sounded in complete control.

She listened again, then looked round sharply at me. 'You can't expect me to drop the money on the ground and walk away. You can forget that. We'll want to see her and know she's safe.'

I guessed that Winston wanted the money on the promise of releasing Virginia later. Tess resisted, her voice calm and hard. Out of the corner of my eye I could see Baker sitting bolt upright in his chair. Every few seconds he combed his fingers through his hair and clutched at his scalp, his hand stretched into a rigid claw.

'It's got to be right,' Tess was saying. 'We're not calling the police so it's going to be just as risky for us. It's got to be right.'

She repeated this a few more times, and eventually she seemed to have argued him round because she told him about the place in Buckinghamshire and started giving him directions.

'I'll be there alone,' she said. 'Just you keep your word.'

For the moment she sounded as if she was the one giving the orders, but when she put the phone down her body slumped as if she was about to collapse and her face was haggard and tearful. She sat down and held her hands over her face, her whole body trembling uncontrollably.

Baker moved across to her and sat on the arm of the chair, putting his arm round her.

'He won't bring her,' she said. 'He says he'll let her go as soon as he gets the money and gets back to London.'

That was the end of my clever ruse. Unless Winston brought her we'd have no chance of getting Virginia away from him, and if he also had the money anything could happen. My feelings must have showed in my face because Tess looked at me with an oddly timid and uncertain smile. 'He'll take the ten thousand.'

I shrugged. Her mouth sagged.

'I just want it to be over with,' she said.

She looked round at Baker as if for support.

'I don't like the easy way he took the bargain,' I told them. 'He might just take the money and try again.'

'What do you think, Roy?' Baker asked.

Tess glared at him, but she avoided looking at Roy.

He hesitated. He looked at me, and when he spoke he sounded nervous and embarrassed.

'It's kind of dodgy. As long as nobody calls the police he's all right.'

He paused. It was a moment of suspense into which Tess interjected a sort of choking sound.

'She can't give him any trouble,' I said, 'if he's got the money to keep her on smack, you know. He could just wait and try again. Do it by instalments.'

There was another uneasy silence.

'We'll see how it goes tomorrow,' Baker said, with a kind of crisp decisiveness which I supposed he used at the office. 'If it all goes wrong we'll have to call in the police.'

His expression belied the tone in which he spoke. His eyes looked off into space as if he was visualising the trouble that decision could cause, and trying to assess the damage.

'If we could find her,' I said, 'it would solve all the problems.'

Baker looked at me impatiently. 'Where would one begin to look?'

'Maybe it's easier than it seems.'

I faced Roy.

'Does he know a lot of people in London?'

'No. We didn't really get a chance to know London. Not like home.'

He meant Manchester. But there was something about the phrase that made Baker shift uncomfortably.

'He's got a cousin. We used to go round there.'

'That's it,' I said. 'He'll want to avoid places Roy knows. That limits his choices. His cousin will be the only person who can help him hide out. If we can find the cousin we've cracked it.'

Roy's expression was sceptical but he said nothing. He was probably thinking about all the little difficulties I'd left out.

'Won't that be dangerous?' Tess asked. Her tone was controlled, the emotions held in careful check. 'You haven't exactly been successful in getting her back so far. What happens if he gets desperate . . .' She let the sentence trail off. She didn't need to finish it.

'We're not blaming you,' Baker said quickly. 'It's just that if he feels threatened he may not go through with the arrangement.'

That was rich, I thought. These two had screwed up the lives of several people, their daughter had worked her way into the sort of trouble they didn't know how to get her out of, and they weren't blaming me. I bit the words back.

'You have to remember,' I said, 'that you're not dealing with a sophisticated gang which has a lot of resources. The guy's more or less on his own, and he needs a lot of money if he's going to get out of this. He needs to solve his problems more than he needs to hurt her. Okay, he's going to use her as a commodity, but that means we've got a hold on him. There's no way he's going to miss out on coming to get that money. That gives us an opportunity, a lot of leeway. You'd be mad not to want to find her. He won't back out.'

Baker nodded at me.

'I think you're right.' He looked down at Tess. 'He's right.'

The words seemed to have given him hope and topped up his confidence all of a sudden. Unexpectedly he smiled. 'Don't worry,' he said to Tess in a wheedling, coaxing voice. She nodded absently in reply.

I looked at Roy, who was watching them expressionlessly.

'That's it then,' I said.

Chapter 25

We had a day and a night in which to find Virginia.

I had left the Bakers' house exuding a confidence I didn't feel. He asked Roy to stay, but the boy said that he had to come along with me.

Baker didn't protest, but both of them had looked at Tess during this exchange with a hint of furtiveness that once again gave me a sense of their resemblance.

In the car I turned to Roy.

'Where to now?'

'Buggered if I know,' he said.

'What do you mean? I thought you knew where to find Winston's cousin.'

'I know where he hangs out,' he said. 'Not where he lives. We used to meet him at a pub, or in the street. You know what I mean?'

I choked down my rage. It wasn't Roy's fault that I'd ignored what I knew about street life and made a stupid assumption.

'All right,' I said. 'Which pub? Which street?'

'No point right now. He'll be sleeping like. Those guys don't move around by day.'

Roy was smirking, as if he pitied my ignorance, and below the surface I could sense a malicious adolescent enjoyment of the situation.

It didn't do much for my temper.

'Cut the teenage rebel shit,' I said. 'I know Winston used to be your mate, but Virginia is your sister, at least that's what you've been telling everybody. So if you're going to help, be bloody helpful or I'll drop you off and do the business myself.'

'All right. Take it easy. I'm just as involved in this as you are.'

He'd stopped smirking, but there was something calculating about the way he looked at me, as if he was trying to gauge my boiling point.

'So what do we do?'

He looked away from me towards the Bakers' house.

'The best thing is to start cruising around about ten. His girls will be out then and he'll be around.'

It was nearly six and whatever we did to locate Winston's cousin would take just as long. I hated the thought of hanging around for four hours but it sounded like the best option.

'You're sure he'll be there?'

He looked at me as if I'd said something peculiar.

'Where would he go?'

As we talked a couple of people had walked past without paying any attention. But in a square like this two black men sitting in a car couldn't be missed and at that moment a tall, thin blonde went by and turned to gaze at us. We gazed right back at her, both giving her the same impassive stare.

'Probably the Neighbourhood Watch,' Roy said softly. 'Cops will be here in a few minutes.'

He made a gesture, but I sat still, feeling a rush of indignation I thought I'd grown out of long ago, and I glared at the woman as she went into a house a few doors away, still glancing back at us.

Suddenly Roy laughed and I laughed with him, certain that he knew what I'd been feeling.

'All right,' I said. 'Let's go.'

Chapter 26

Driving across Chelsea Bridge I remembered the way Roy and Baker had been. Every once in a while their eyes had met and then they'd been intent, mutually absorbed and searching. Like two lovers, or two deadly opponents perhaps.

In between it was oddly touching to see how hard they tried to disguise their fascination with each other. Even so, Roy's mood would change from time to time and he'd say something sarcastic. Then he'd laugh in that sneering tone of his and Baker's mouth would go small and tight.

'How do you feel about Baker now?' I asked Roy.

'I don't know.'

'What are you going to do?'

'I don't know. I'll see when this gets sorted.'

I wondered how long that would take. I didn't say what I was thinking to Roy, but it struck me that getting Virginia back was probably the easiest part of the deal. After that they'd all be back to normal and the Bakers' normal life didn't include Roy.

He didn't speak again until I'd put the key in the door of my flat and then it was only to tell me that the phone was ringing. I had heard it before he did, and I sprinted up the stairs.

I was half expecting it to be the Bakers with bad news. Pictures of Virginia, with dead, half-open eyes, in the grainy black and white of newspaper print, kept flashing through my mind all the way up, and when I picked up the phone and heard Sophie's voice I didn't know whether to be relieved or angry.

'The answer is yes,' she said. 'We can be together tonight.'

I just stopped myself from swearing aloud. I'd forgotten the message I left her.

'I'm sorry,' I told her, 'since I left that message something's come up. I can't make it.'

She was silent for a moment.

'What's so important?'

For a moment I wished I could tell her, but the fact that she was asking irritated me.

'Some work I'm doing.'

'Something to do with Virginia?'

Too many questions, and I definitely didn't want to tell her.

'Why?' I asked innocently. 'Have you seen her?'

Another silence.

'I'm sorry Sophie,' I said. 'Things are a little difficult now, but I'll talk to you about it when I see you. I'll telephone you in a couple of days.'

At the other end she made an impatient noise.

'I don't know,' she said. 'I like you but this mysteriousness brings back bad memories.'

'All right Sophie,' I said. I was trying to sound conciliatory because what she'd said about the bad memories was probably the literal truth. 'It's really nothing mysterious. Just work. I'll explain when I see you.'

After she'd said goodbye I stood there for a moment listening to the tone. Right then I didn't have the time and seeing her would have been a distraction in any case, but in a few days I'd probably be sorry.

I looked round at Roy. He had been listening, but now his eyes were closed and he seemed to be drifting off to sleep. At rest his face had the blank, open air of a child.

That reminded me. I picked up the phone again and rang my son. Friday was one of my days to see him and I'd forgotten that too.

His mother answered, and I told her that I was tied up for the evening.

'I wish you wouldn't do this,' she said. 'He's been waiting for the phone to ring, and he'll be so disappointed. The thing is, he only takes it out on me.'

My heart sagged with guilt, but something told me that this was precisely the effect she was after.

'I'm sorry,' I said, 'but I think he'll understand. Let me speak to him.'

When he came on the line he didn't sound too devastated.

'What's happening, Dad?'

'I won't be around tonight,' I told him. 'I've got a job to do.'

'When can I come?'

I told him I didn't know but I'd get in touch over the weekend. He didn't sound upset, but after I put down the phone I found myself wondering whether he was merely concealing his feelings.

I looked at Roy again. He had slumped down in the armchair and was snoring slightly. Seeing him like this, his body slack and vulnerable, made me wonder once again what would happen to him.

Then it hit me. Here I was worrying about other people's children when I didn't even know what my son was thinking. If I had any sense, I thought, I would pack it in and go see him. Why me, I thought.

All at once, though, the ghastly pictures of a slaughtered Virginia flashed back into my mind. Some instinct was telling me that if I dropped out at this stage everything would go wrong, and in a couple of days I'd read about it in the papers and feel sick. For my own peace of mind I had to go through with it.

The idea made me feel churned up and angry with myself. So I slammed into the kitchen, flung open the window, leaned out, and in an effort to restore my calm, began taking deep breaths of the exhaust fumes which filled the quiet evening air.

Chapter 27

'You're going too fast,' he said suddenly. 'Slow down.'

I slowed down. We were in Edgware Road and he began peering through the windscreen. Winston's cousin Rodney hung out in this area, and Roy was certain we'd locate him sooner or later.

In a little while we turned off and drove through Sussex Gardens, past a line of cheap hotels. The neon signs picked out a series of pretentious names. Imperial. Viceroy. But the flickering colours gave them a garishness which put me in mind of a fifties 'B' movie.

Some girls were already standing on the corners waiting for customers. As the car cruised past they looked up hopefully. Most of them seemed young, in their teens, and slightly grubby.

'Rodney has a couple of these girls,' Roy said. 'Maybe they're not out yet though.'

We pulled round the corner, went past Paddington Station and stopped. It was still early and there were knots of people moving in and out of the station and along the pavements. A small group of teenagers came past us, speaking loud German. By coincidence they were all fair-haired and they had the carefree look of people on holiday.

Funny, I told Roy, that the first sight so many young people from abroad would have of London was this area, with its sleazy hotels, villains and prostitutes.

144

'It's not so bad,' he said, but I could tell from his absent tone that he was thinking about something else.

I wondered whether Winston was on his mind. I had to remind myself that they were friends and had depended on each other. Now, by the looks of it, they were on opposite sides of the fence. Roy had a lot to think about.

I had a feeling I could read some of his thoughts.

Boys like Roy trained themselves to prey on the world. When you started out at the bottom, hard work and good behaviour just bought you more of what you already had. The only way to get what you wanted was to take it away from someone else. Sometimes you had to pay a price but that was how it was.

Now, more or less by accident he looked like gaining a foothold in a world where everything he wanted was there for the taking, and I was willing to bet that underneath all the conflict about his parentage, his mind was busily chasing around the problem of how to exploit it.

I had a few things on my own mind. When I made the suggestion about going out to the Bakers' cottage in Buckinghamshire I'd had vague thoughts about wrestling Virginia away.

He wasn't going to take her with him so that was out, but at least the meeting would take him away for the whole of the evening, and that would give us a chance to locate her, without the added problem of battling with his ton of bulging muscles.

'Let's go to the pub,' Roy said. 'We've probably got a while to wait.'

We got out and walked around the corner to the nearest pub. It wasn't too far off closing time and the pub was crowded and noisy.

It had the sort of decor which went well with the area. The walls were covered with a red flock paper which reflected the motifs in the maroon carpet. The lamps were glass globes with heraldic animals etched on them, and two massive chandeliers hovered over the wooden bar.

The place seemed an odd setting for its clientele, a weird mix of late commuters and travellers, elderly locals, dreadlocks and their girls, and a carousing group of young white people clustered round the jukebox.

145

I ordered Special Brew without asking Roy. It had to be his drink. Beside me three pensioners were arguing loudly. They all wore presentable dark suits and clean, open-collared shirts, but the clothes hung flapping on their old bones, and the pint glasses in front of them looked as if they'd been nursed to the point of lethargy.

'She's a dirty old cow,' one of them said angrily. 'I'll tell you what she bleeding does. Every time one of the old corgis has a shit on the carpet, she just puts a newspaper over it, and bloody leaves it there. The maids have to clean it up, don't they?'

'How do you know that, then?'

The old man who asked the question had a flat cap on, and his eyes under its brim were sceptical.

The first old man sounded even angrier when he replied. 'I've been told, haven't I? Dirty old cow.'

'Yah,' sneered his friend in the flat hat. 'You're bleeding mad, you are.'

I paid for the drinks and pushed my way back through the crowd to where Roy was standing. The jukebox was playing a reggae number and the music was too loud for an easy conversation, so we simply stood there.

To one side of us the group of young whites shouted against the noise of the jukebox. There were about a dozen of them and they looked as if they did some sort of low-level bureaucratic jobs. Town hall employees, I guessed.

Suddenly a tall, slender girl with long dark hair, wearing a black dress and a red cardigan, stepped in front of one of the white boys, and holding out a card began reading verses in a loud voice. It was something about his birthday, and as she read she took off the cardigan and placed it on the floor, then she took off the dress and pressed closer to him.

She was wearing a tiny black camisole which was cut high at the back so you could see her bare cheeks above the black stockings, and the man began gripping and squeezing busily. The girl continued, slipping down the garment at the front. The man's hands grew frantic, each one now operating as if independently, groping at everything within reach.

The girl read on, holding the card high to see what it said, leaning back so that the man could fumble at her breasts, then with the other hand she slid the camisole right down and stepped out of it to a roar of applause. She kicked the cloth away and threw her arms wide apart.

'Happy birthday,' she shouted, and began hugging and kissing him.

Around them the man's friends clapped and shouted their approval. The women in the party looked on prune-faced, or turned away and talked to each other. In a moment the show was over and the girl picked up her clothes and walked quickly over to the ladies.

I met Roy's eyes.

'That's put at least a year on his life,' he said.

The bell for last orders had gone twice while we watched the little scene, and the barmen were now calling time. The pub began to empty slowly. Outside, it was still a warm night and we drove back through the district with the windows down. Roy scanned the pavements intently. Still nothing.

'Wouldn't he be around by now if he was going to be?' I asked him.

The thought that we might not find him kept surfacing from the back of my mind and each time I thought about what might be happening to Virginia.

'It's early yet. Sometimes they don't get out till later.' He sounded almost nonchalant about it, but his eyes kept on searching.

At the top end of Edgware Road I turned left past Marble Arch.

'Where are we going?'

'The Palm Grove,' I told him.

'Winston won't be there.'

'Not Winston. Something else.'

Something else was the Boss. As we drove along it had struck me that Winston might have set up another deal with Goonay's friends. That would explain the way that he'd gone for what money he could get without too much quibbling. The date of the transaction would determine how much time he had, or how much time we had.

I couldn't begin to guess what he'd do with Virginia, but I had a nasty suspicion that the affair wouldn't end when he got the money. He had nothing to lose by holding on to her, and he was sure to know that the Bakers could kick in a lot more than ten thousand if they were pushed. If things worked out that way he might give her an overdose and walk away.

Whether the deal was going forward and when, were sure to be important in any case, but the only way I could think of finding out was through the Boss. It was gone eleven and he'd be in the Palm Grove, showing off his jewellery.

Roy looked at me curiously, but he didn't ask any more and I didn't explain. If it didn't work out I would have wasted time we could hardly afford, and if it all ended in disaster I didn't want him to remember that fact too clearly.

Chapter 28

The Palm Grove looked exactly the same, as if no one had left or entered since I'd been there last, and I was just beginning to look around for the Boss when I saw him standing by the bar.

This time he was wearing a red suit and a blue shirt with ruffles down the front. He spotted me as I came up to him with Roy following close behind, and his expression turned coyly severe.

'Boss,' I said. 'What's happening, man?'

He tilted his head to look at me out of the corner of his eye.

'You blood,' he said, drawing the word out.

'What's wrong?'

'What's wrong? You know what's wrong. You called my name to my Apache friend.'

I had forgotten mentioning him to Goonay.

'Don't worry, man. He knew.'

'You shouldn't call a man's name.'

'Boss,' I said. I knew the game. He would be stern and dignified. I would be placatory until face was saved.

'Boss, I'm sorry. But you know why that happened. There wasn't anything else I could do.'

'Chah.'

He hadn't changed his pose since I'd spoken to him and I knew from every inflexible line of his body that he was enjoying himself immensely.

'A drink for the Boss,' I told the barman. 'Whatever he wants.'

There was a lager standing in front of him, but when the barman raised his eyebrows, the Boss pushed it away grandly.

'Double vodka on the rocks.'

I figured then that honour was more or less satisfied. The Boss had recognised Roy standing on the other side of me and I could see that his curiosity was piqued. I leaned closer so we couldn't be heard.

'I found the guy I was looking for, you know.'

The Boss raised his eyebrows at Roy. His expression was dubious.

'I got everything under control,' I told him. 'The only thing is I need a little help with something.'

The Boss looked at me with stagy contempt.

'Don't ask me,' he said. 'I don't want to get mixed up in your business.'

The vodka had arrived and he picked it up and swirled it around as if he was guessing the vintage. I took his elbow and moved him away from the bar.

'Come. Come. Let's talk.'

He shook my hand off, but he moved with me to a quiet corner, smiling a little superciliously, the great star listening to an importunate henchman. Roy stayed where he was. He still didn't know what it was all about but he knew enough to recognise fancy footwork when he saw it.

'Is no mixing up,' I told the Boss. 'The guys' deal got fucked the other night, and I must know whether it's going down again.'

'So you can fuck it up again?'

'Come on, Boss. It's important. Swear to God that you won't come into it at all. I just want to know when it's happening. I don't even want to know where.'

The Boss looked more supercilious than ever.

'Why ask me? I don't know anything about these people, boy. I want to keep my health and my pretty face you know. I don't get mixed up in these things.'

'No mixing up, Boss,' I said. 'But I'm going to bet you that you could tell me something.'

I felt in my pocket. I had a twenty and a five. I took the twenty out and folded it lengthways, then I poked it into the outside pocket of the red suit. The Boss looked down at it without moving.

'You'll have to bet more than that,' he said.

I made up my mind.

'Wait for me,' I said.

I went out without saying any more and climbed the stairs to the pavement. I saw Roy coming after me as I went, but I waved him back and he disappeared.

There was a bank with a cash machine not too far away from the entrance and I walked there rapidly. As I dialled fifty a little party of Americans walked past, and when I looked at them they averted their eyes quickly. Too streetwise, I thought, even to look at a black man at night.

Back inside the club the Boss hadn't moved. I walked up to him and poked two more twenties into the pocket. The first one had disappeared.

'My Apache friend,' he said immediately, 'is financing my recording. I have to do the mix this week and he told me to pick up some duns day after tomorrow. He said things would be cool that day.'

I supposed this meant that the deal would be on for tomorrow.

'Thanks Boss,' I said.

'What for? I don't know nothing.'

He turned away and paced back to the bar. I waved at Roy and moved for the stairs. I felt like running. I couldn't work out exactly what that piece of news had changed but it seemed obvious that once the deal was made Winston would have to take a number of decisions. I had little hope that he would release Virginia, so it was now crucial to locate her before he had to make up his mind what to do.

'What was all that about then?' Roy asked as we drove round Marble Arch.

I told him and he nodded thoughtfully.

'We're still looking for Rodney?'

My control snapped and I snarled at him, 'Of course we bloody are. What else have we got?'

In the half-light of the car I could feel him looking at me.

'What are you getting out of this?' he said.

His tone was a little puzzled as if he'd been wondering about that for a long time.

I considered the question. Times and things had changed. But

151

once I had got involved it was almost impossible to escape. I glanced at Roy. I had got into this out of curiosity, sheer nosiness, but it was also to do with the way he had become identified in my mind with my son. Now I knew him it was different. Yet somewhere deep down I felt that what happened to him was something to do with me.

There were so many times and places, I thought, where blacks and whites met in a desperate whirlpool of rage, exploitation, fear. Roy had experienced his life in the middle of all this. I knew what that was like and perhaps I could do something about it. But even if I couldn't I had to try.

Somehow I couldn't say any of this to Roy.

'It's a job, you know. I said I'd do it, and I'm going to see the end of it.'

He nodded.

'He's paying you?'

Now he was worrying about Dad's money.

'Not that much, I wouldn't think.' I smiled at him. 'You rich folks didn't get rich by spreading it about you know.'

He chuckled, as if the remark had tickled him.

'Not me. I wouldn't know about that.'

The space between us was easier and I was going to say something else about how I felt when Roy gave a grunting exclamation and pointed.

'There she is.'

'Who?'

'Hazel. Rodney's main lady.'

She looked the part. Beginners just down from the North usually wore clothes which were functional in intent, skirts and trousers which could be lifted and lowered easily. More experienced girls with a sense of professional pride, dressed with a feeling for showbiz glitz.

Hazel was obviously the experienced sort.

She was standing with three other girls on the pavement near the all-night shop, and she was wearing a red leather suit with high-heeled red sandals and black mesh stockings. Her hair was pulled back into a long dark braid, threaded through with a thin red ribbon.

'What are you going to do?' I asked Roy.

As far as I was concerned he could handle this one.

'Nothing,' he said. 'Pull up by the corner. We'll just keep our eyes on her and wait.'

'How do you know we're not wasting our time? He doesn't have to turn up, you know.'

Roy gave me a small 'leave this to me' smile.

'She's the head lady, man. She sorts the others out. Gets the money together and that. If there's any trouble she sorts that out that and all. They don't really need him unless something heavy happens. She rings him regularly, and he comes round once or twice just to see how things are going, especially if he needs some money. If he's short. He doesn't hang about you know, because of the cops, but he's bound to see her or she's bound to go and see him some time tonight.'

I nodded at him. 'We'll wait.'

From where we sat near the corner we could see the little group of women through the back window. Every few minutes a car pulled up and one of them got in. Hazel was like a general marshalling her troops, sending them off one by one until only she was left. Then she began pacing towards the corner but before she could get there a red Cortina drew up. She leaned on the window for a moment, talking to the driver, then got in. I looked at Roy.

'It's only a customer,' he said.

'Can't afford to lose her.'

He nodded, and I started the engine and moved after them.

By now the traffic was thin and it wasn't difficult to follow the steady red lights. The car turned left in a short while and headed for the warren of back streets and alleyways behind Paddington Station. I followed at a distance feeling oddly exhilarated by the chase.

'Stay back,' Roy muttered.

I slowed down. We were the only two cars moving along these deserted little streets, and I let them get well ahead. But in a moment the red car turned a corner and disappeared. I speeded up again, but when we reached the turn the street was empty.

I swore aloud. If we lost her and she was meeting Rodney we'd miss him.

'Keep going slow,' Roy said.

We crawled, although my feet itched to plunge on the

accelerator. I was just about to speed up again, when Roy touched my arm.

'There.'

We had just passed the entrance to a darkened cul-de-sac. I stopped and pulled into the pavement. We looked back. I had a feeling that there was another opening to the passage, just too small for a car.

'I'll take a look,' I said. 'Just in case we're missing something.'

Roy nodded and I got out and walked back softly.

The street was short and narrow, lined with small shops. At this time it was deserted and my footsteps seemed to echo resoundingly off the front of the buildings, as I reached the corner and peered cautiously round it.

The alleyway ran between high brick walls. At some point it had given access to a few small factories but now they were gone. Up above only a couple of tiny bathroom windows looked down into the alley.

The car was drawn up close to the brick wall on the left. Hazel stood, bending over to lean with her elbows on the bonnet, her skirt up around her waist, her feet planted wide apart and her thighs gleaming white above the dark stockings.

Behind her the fair-haired man who had been driving the car was pumping rapidly back and forth, his hands clasping her grinding buttocks.

It was an eerie, somehow surrealist scene, the dark and empty alley, with the only points of light seeming to concentrate and reflect off Hazel's thighs and the man's pale face and hair.

I retreated quietly and got back into the car.

'It's just a customer,' I told Roy.

In less than ten minutes we were back in the main road, watching Hazel emerge demurely from the red car to be greeted by one of the other women who had returned while we were away.

The night wore on. Over the next hour Hazel went to a hotel, then into a nearby block of flats with two Arabs, then back to the alley. The fourth time Roy and I stayed where we were, and she was back in about twenty minutes.

After a couple of hours of this, the women seemed to be taking a break. The entire group moved away from the roadside and went into the shop, then emerged and crossed the road to

154

the phone box. One of them went in and began making a call, the others loitered outside, drinking from the cans they'd just bought.

'Checking on the kids,' Roy said.

Suddenly Hazel faced the street and waved. Somehow I knew without looking that Rodney had arrived.

Roy nudged me. 'The Jag. The Jag. Rodney.'

The blue-grey Jaguar pulled up beside the phone booth and Rodney got out. He had locks which swung almost down to his shoulders and he was dressed in jeans, sneakers and a short brown leather jacket which had diagonal fawn streaks across the front. He had a body like a good sprinter in training, muscular and agile at the same time, and he looked as formidable as Winston, although in a very different way.

The women stood in a little cluster in front of him, like a row of schoolkids greeting a parent, then after a few minutes they began strolling out of sight around the corner.

'They'll be back in a minute,' Roy said.

He was right. In a short while they reappeared. Rodney was walking ahead of the others with Hazel, and when they reached the car the two of them got in. For a moment I thought Rodney was taking Hazel with him and I switched the engine on, but the Jag didn't move.

'He won't be long,' Roy said.

As he spoke the Jag's rear lights began to glow and Hazel got out. As soon as she slammed the door shut Rodney roared abruptly into a U-turn and sped past us before I could react. Luckily the traffic lights were red or he'd have been gone before I could move. As I pulled out after him I could feel Roy watching with a grin.

'All right,' I muttered. 'Nobody's perfect.'

As it turned out Rodney's speed on the turn was a false alarm. He drove at a fairly sedate pace down towards Notting Hill. I kept what I thought was a safe distance between us, but by now it was early morning and there weren't many other cars on the road. It wasn't difficult to keep him in sight.

We turned into one of the streets between Notting Hill and Westbourne Grove, and now Rodney pulled up in front of a house. He got out and went in with a springing gait that reminded me of the way he had taken off in the car.

I drove past and parked further up on the same side.

'What now?' I asked Roy.

'I'll go and ask him if Winston's around.'

'Just like that?'

'Just like that.'

He grinned at me.

'If Winston's talked to him lately he'll tell you bugger all.'

'I know, but at least that will tell us if Winston's been in touch.'

'What good will that do?'

He looked at me irritably but he didn't answer.

I slammed my hand on the steering wheel. I was as irritated with myself as he probably was. I'd been stupid in not working out a plan for dealing with Rodney. But the impact seemed to clear my mind.

'All right,' I said. 'Let's both go.'

'That will put him off.'

'Maybe. But we can start off by assuming he's heard from Winston. If you go and talk to him alone it won't bother him too much. They'll probably expect you to be looking for Winston. But if I'm also there, shooting my mouth off, it's bound to puzzle Rodney. At least. He'll need to tell Winston that there's a new element in the situation. Some strange geezer knocking around with you. Maybe they'll think it's Old Bill even. It's worth it. If we mess him about a bit he'll go and tell Winston and when he does we'll be watching. You know what I mean? The shadow misses nothing, man.'

He still looked sceptical but while I'd been talking I had become more enthusiastic about the plan.

'Creative improvisation,' I told him.

'We'll probably improvise ourselves right into the shite house,' he said. Then he laughed abruptly. 'But you're right. We don't have anything to lose.'

I laughed with him. We seemed, all of a sudden, and at the same time, to have worked ourselves into a light-headed and reckless mood.

That probably accounted for the coolness with which I was standing in front of Rodney's door, ringing his doorbell as hard as I could.

'My life is full of doors lately,' I told Roy, 'with something unpleasant behind them.'

156

Before he could reply the door opened and Rodney was standing there. He made a sound halfway between a grunt and a growl.

'All right,' I said. 'Nice to see you too.'

His eyes rested on me briefly, then returned to Roy.

Close up he was taller than either of us, and although he wasn't as big as Winston, he had a muscular presence which seemed to fill the space around him. His eyes looked odd, with a dull, intense glow somewhere behind their flat surfaces.

'Winston here?'

Rodney shook his head slowly and his locks moved like lazy snakes.

'I want to see him,' Roy said.

His voice had an aggressive edge. It had been clear from the first moment that Rodney, even allowing for his style, wasn't about to greet us with open arms. Winston must have been in touch, so there was no point in trying to be smooth.

Rodney smiled as if Roy had said something funny. He leaned sideways on the wall next to him.

'Maybe he don't want to see you,' he said.

'Listen,' I said. 'You don't have to be afraid of us. We just want to talk to him. If he keeps hold of that girl he could be in serious trouble.'

This time he let his eyes stay on me. I had deliberately used key words like 'afraid' and 'serious trouble'. The first suggested an insult, the second carried echoes of policemen and courts.

His expression changed only a little, but I saw in it a menace so real that I almost moved back a pace, in spite of myself.

'Fuck off,' he said quietly.

He began pushing the door closed, but I already had my foot in the corner of it.

Rodney looked down, then looked back up at me, and in the same movement reached into his back pocket, then seemingly without a break in the smooth flow of the gesture, slashed at my face. I hadn't seen the knife. All I could remember later was his hand coming at me faster than I could think. But Roy had reacted quicker. Even before my reflexes had begun to work, he had grabbed my jacket and pulled me out of the line of Rodney's hand as it swept across.

We ended up halfway down the steps, tumbling over

ourselves to get further down, and when I looked up again, Rodney had disappeared and the door was shut.

We walked quickly away from the house. I said nothing because I didn't trust myself to speak. I was in a state of suffocating rage, compounded by the mounting realisation that he would have cut me badly if Roy hadn't pulled me out of the way. My knees trembled and I had difficulty in controlling my legs as we walked. I was no stranger to violence but I was unnerved by the silent speed and vicious decisiveness of Rodney's actions. Unexpectedly, I felt humiliated.

'Thanks,' I told Roy. 'He'd have sliced me up for sure if you hadn't moved so fast.'

He grinned cheerfully at me. The whole incident seemed to have amused him.

'Next time you start fucking around with guys like that, just remember they take life serious.'

He laughed. I couldn't share the joke, but I nodded.

'I'll remember.'

I slumped back gratefully into the car. I seemed to have been awake for a long time. It was that period of the night, just before the first patch of grey began to appear in the sky, when everything was quiet and dark, and even the cars looked asleep.

Beside me Roy was still smiling.

'Wait?' he asked.

I looked around at him, a little surprised by his coolness. At the same time I was grateful. In the past I'd worked with people who would have been reduced to quivering wrecks by five minutes' unpunctuality. One thing to be said for an insecure life, I thought, was that you didn't panic.

'We might as well wait,' I said. 'Let's see if he goes running to Winston.'

'Suppose he telephones.'

'Maybe. We'll just have to wait and see. But I've got a feeling Rodney won't like using the phone for private business, even if there's one where Winston's hanging out.'

Roy nodded, then he turned around and began climbing over into the back seat. 'Better keep your head down,' he said, 'in case he comes this way.'

I stretched out across the front seat so that I could see back to Rodney's car without being seen.

The next thing I was conscious of was Roy's voice.

'Come on,' he said. 'He's moving.'

It was like driving in a dream at first, but luckily he simply drove back towards Edgware Road. Once there, he stopped near the phone booth where Hazel had been standing earlier on. She was still there, on her own this time, and as soon as he pulled up she climbed in and he zoomed off again. He turned and came past us. I stared straight ahead, hoping that he wasn't looking. Behind me I could hear Roy scrunching down into the back seat.

'You think he saw us?'

'I don't know,' I said. 'I hope not.'

I had the sneaky feeling that Rodney didn't give a toss, either because he was too confident or because he had nothing to hide, but in any case he drove sedately back towards Paddington. This time he went under the motorway and held on into Harrow Road. A little way down he stopped and let Hazel out. She walked down the passageway towards a block of flats, moving tiredly, swaying on her high heels.

Rodney drove on, then turned left at the police station and emerged on the other side of Notting Hill.

'Bugger's only going home again,' I told Roy.

He swore in disgust, but just as I was wondering what to do next, Rodney rolled past the turning where his house was and vanished round the next corner.

I sped after him and we were just in time to see him pull up, right behind Winston's car.

'Get down,' I hissed at Roy, and drove past as fast as I dared. But Rodney wasn't looking around. He simply walked across the pavement and let himself into a house on the right.

It had an estate agent's board up in front which said it was a partly occupied investment. Like hell it was.

I'd seen that board up for over three months. The windows on two of the floors were boarded up and only the top floor sported some limp and dirty curtains. For a moment I had an irrational desire to laugh because it was the sort of place which my son, his imagination nourished by kids' fiction, would have readily identified as a kidnapper's den. But I would have kept on driving past it without a second glance.

'Got him,' I said. 'Winston's there and Virginia must be with him.'

'In the next street all the time. After all that.'

I pulled round the next corner and stopped. I felt fully awake now.

'We'll wait till he goes off to meet Tess, then we'll go in.'

'Why not now?'

'Come on man. You want to go in while Winston and Rodney are there? You feeling lucky? And just suppose she's not there after all.'

Roy nodded. 'All right. But suppose she's not there anyway?'

'Don't think it,' I said. 'If she's not there we're in big trouble.'

Chapter 29

In the end I decided not to wait. It was a good bet that Winston wouldn't be going anywhere till he had to meet Tess. I switched the engine on and let the car find its way home.

I gave Roy the bed, and lay on the floor on top of my son's sleeping bag. I had put the TV on to catch the news but the twittering voices irritated me so much that I got up and turned it off. The world that these bright-eyed personalities presented had no room for terror and despair that lasted longer than a few minutes. We had spent the night in a very different sort of place and the contrast was too much for me.

My dreams were full of monsters, and the ringing of the telephone dragged me from the bottom of a black pit. I had a pain in my hip, my head hurt from somewhere deep in my skull, my eyes ached as if they'd been boiled and replaced in their sockets, and I felt I'd never manage to reach the phone in time. But it kept on ringing as I crawled across the floor to it.

It was Tess Baker. I told her we'd found Winston.

'Did you see Virginia? Was she there?'

I told her we didn't know for certain. There was a silence.

'We think she's probably there,' I said. 'What time did you say you'd see our friend?'

'At midnight.'

She must have been indulging some hidden sense of drama when she fixed the time. It didn't have to be as late as all that.

'We'll come about seven.'

'What are you going to do?' She sounded shrill and anxious.

'We'll talk about it when I get there. We'll keep watching the place in case there's any movement.'

'Can't you come earlier? We don't know what's happening.'

'There's nothing to tell. Really there isn't, but I'll call you later in any case.'

She seemed to accept that, and I put the phone down. It was a relief to stop talking to her. The jagged edges of her nerves kept poking through the surface of her manners, and it was disturbing.

I lay back, thinking about what we had to do later. I had the sense that we had no way of controlling what came next, and what I really wanted to do was to sit in my flat with a book and a cup of tea till it was all over.

It was gone one o'clock so I got up and went into the kitchen. I banged on the bedroom door as I went by and I thought I heard a faint groan. A few minutes later Roy emerged.

'Heard anything?'

I shook my head.

'I thought I heard the phone.'

'You did.'

I told him about the phone call and he listened without comment.

Outside the window the horns of the city honked and hollered. There was a little clutch of parking spaces for motor cycles just down the road, and the messengers' radios squawked and blared out instructions from time to time.

I told Roy that we'd have to go and keep an eye on Winston's place. He nodded. He looked a bit fed up. For a moment I found myself falling back into a habit I'd had with my son, looking anxiously at his expression to see how he felt, planning how to make it better. This morning Roy looked young, a child with clear eyes and no bad thoughts.

'Don't worry,' I said. 'It will all be over soon.'

He nodded again, looked at me, then looked away. 'Those pictures in the bedroom.' He gestured with his thumb. 'It's your son?'

'That's right. Young master himself.'

'He looks like a good kid.'

'The best.'

He paused as if thinking out what he was going to say. His glance met mine and skittered away.

'I don't understand that guy. He's too much you know.'

'Who's that?'

I knew who, but I wanted him to say it. I could see that for some reason he wanted to unburden himself, to talk. I really didn't want to look inside the box of problems that was his head, and I knew that if it came to advice I wouldn't know what to say, but I didn't have it in me to stop him.

'Baker.'

He said the name reluctantly.

'Your father. You've said it often enough. Don't you feel like he's your dad?'

He shrugged.

'I suppose so. I was thinking about it last night. There used to be times when all I wanted to do was see him and smash his face in. But then I didn't know who he was.'

He gave a short, barking laugh. I smiled to keep him company. The other side of the coin, I figured, was probably that he had also wanted to put his arms round him and cry on his shoulder, and I wondered whether he'd broken down in that way when they had their private talk.

'Maybe after all this is over, he'll tell me to piss off again.'

He laughed, but he was watching me narrowly, as if trying to assess my response.

I shook my head.

'It's all too late for that,' I said. 'He'll have to try and sort things out with you and Virginia all at the same time. It's all connected and he knows it. Maybe it will be difficult for him because of his wife. I mean, give him a shot at working it out.'

He nodded. 'She don't like me.'

'You can't say that. You don't know her. People like that are funny, you've got to know them to understand their reactions, and anyway it's all bound to be a bit of a shock to her.'

I hoped that he wouldn't remember that she had known about him for a long time, and that Baker's behaviour had probably been shaped and guided by Tess.

'Maybe,' he said. 'But he's kind of henpecked, eh?'

He laughed again, but he wasn't joking. It was odd. Something about his mood told me that he wasn't just anxious about his status. Somewhere in there lurked a genuine concern for Baker. In whatever peculiar way that such a thing was possible for him, he'd started to feel like the man's son.

'It's a funny thing,' he said. 'I always used to think that my dad must be an important man. I really believed that. Now I see him and he's a rich MP and that and I can't believe it.'

I didn't answer. I was tired of it all and I thought that perhaps if I didn't encourage him he'd change the subject.

'Do you think I can trust him?'

He seemed to be asking himself the question.

'I don't see why not,' I said.

I glanced at him, but he was looking away. Suddenly I was irritated.

'Suppose you have to make a choice between your dad and Winston?'

'Winston's nothing to do with it.'

'But suppose. It might happen.'

He shrugged sullenly. 'I don't know.'

'They say blood's thicker than water.'

'Maybe,' he said.

Chapter 30

I dropped Roy off at the bookie's on the corner of the road near Notting Hill. From the door he could just see the house where we thought Winston was, and the big custom car was still parked in front.

Before I drove off I gave him some money to entertain himself, and a paper to pick out the runners.

'I might catch a few winners,' he said. 'It might be my turn today.'

'It might. Just leave the dogs alone.'

Without Roy I felt lighter, as if a burden had come off my back. I drove fast towards St John's Wood.

My son lived in that direction. He should be hanging around the garden or the park. If I was quick I might catch him. When I thought about seeing him it was as if some physical craving asserted itself.

I plunged on through the sunlit afternoon feeling a thrill of anticipation.

In the event I didn't get as far as the house. I was going past the little park nearby when I caught sight of him, standing in a big triangle with a couple of other boys kicking a football around.

One of the boys was black, the other white. My first thought was that this was a strange coincidence. Then I remembered that in most of inner London this was a more or less usual combination.

As I watched, my son caught the ball on his foot, kicked it up and down a couple of times, flicked it over his head and back-heeled it to one of his chums. His movements had such a liquid fluency that I pulled into the side of the road in a state of disbelieving pride.

He looked round as I got out of the car and walked towards the gate.

'There's my dad,' I heard him shout.

He reached me as I came in through the iron railings and threw his arms round my waist. I lifted him, swung him round and put him down. As I did so he punched me hard in the stomach and I collapsed dramatically.

'That hurt,' I gasped.

I was only exaggerating a little. He was getting to be a big boy. Behind him I could see his friends standing by, smiling vaguely, waiting to get on with the game. He was taller and stronger and better looking than both of them, I thought. He was better looking than most kids, I thought.

He helped me up, still laughing at my paternal antics.

'Wanna play, Dad?'

I did want to play, and for the next hour or so I scampered around feeling only delight in the sunlight and being alive and being with him.

Afterwards we walked home, bouncing the ball between us.

'What would you do,' I asked him, 'if you had to do something dangerous to help a friend?'

'Is this a trick?'

'No.'

'Really dangerous?'

'Yes.'

He considered.

'I'd still do it, but I'd be careful.'

'All right, but if that ever happens tell me or your mum before you do anything. Understand?'

'Yes. Are you working on an article, Dad?'

'Something like it.'

We had reached his house and he grabbed me round the waist and hugged me for a moment, laying his head against my chest in the old baby gesture. Then he was gone.

I drove back, fantasising about his chances. Perhaps one day he'd play for England, or win an event at the Olympics. On the whole I thought I preferred the Olympics.

I was so preoccupied with stuff like this that I nearly drove past the bookie's. Roy must have been watching for me, because as soon as I stopped by the pavement he dashed out and ducked into the car.

'Had a good day?' I asked him. 'Did you draw at all?'

In reply he took a bundle of notes out of his pocket and peeled some off into my hand, about twice what I'd given him.

'You drew,' I said. 'Looks like you gave that bookie some licks.'

'Nearly killed him, man. I couldn't stop winning. This is a lucky day for me. Real lucky. I think my luck's turned.'

I was going to say something about hoping it would keep up, but when I glanced over at him I could see that he meant it. The experience had been special to him, and I didn't want to spoil it with sarcasm. Besides I was hoping it was true. Like gamblers, people living at the bottom of the ladder believe in luck. What else is there? We could use it in the night ahead, I thought.

Winston's car was still parked where it had been before.

'See anything?'

'Rodney's been in and out a couple of times. But that's all.'

'What about Winston?'

He shook his head. 'Nothing.'

He gave me a moody look. 'If it wasn't for all this,' he said, 'I'd have sorted it out with Winston.'

'What are you on about?' I said. 'This is the guy who beat the hell out of you and left you tied up and bleeding on the floor.'

He shrugged. 'He saved me from worse inside. When we had the sitdown in the Scrubs he took on three screws who were going to do me over. Without him I'd probably have died. He treated me better than my own family.'

'So what are you going to do? You want him to get away with it?'

He shook his head.

'No. Not any more. But I won't let them send him away. Don't you try it.'

'Nobody going to send anybody away, man. Everybody's been conspiring like bloody mad. Grass one, grass the lot. You should know that.'

167

He smiled faintly. 'Yes.'

'Let's go get some chips.'

My way of ending the conversation. I opened the car door, then changed my mind, closed it and put the car in gear. Roy sat back in his seat without comment and I drove off. There wasn't much point in hanging around. We had to see the Bakers, and it would be better to get back here early so as to watch for Winston's departure.

Roy was silent as we drove through the afternoon traffic. Perhaps he was thinking about what he'd said. I was. It struck me that the conflicts in his loyalties would tear him apart sooner or later, if not this time. Any time he came down on one side or the other it would feel like a betrayal. The choices he would have to make were impossible, but he'd have to make them.

We crawled up to the Bakers' place in a heavy silence. Baker himself opened the door, and behind him the house seemed filled with a sort of muffled hush, as if someone had died and they were waiting for the undertaker.

A red leather briefcase was sitting on the table in the big room that looked out on to the garden. Tess sat next to it, and she greeted us with an inclination of the head. The french windows were open and the curtains wide apart to admit the late sunshine, but it didn't make the room any more cheerful. From here the evening seemed like a melancholy prelude to the night.

'I'll be leaving as soon as the traffic slackens,' Tess said. 'In about an hour and a half.'

I looked at my watch. It was nearly seven.

'It won't take you three hours, will it?'

'I want to get there early,' she said. 'We haven't been there for a while. There are some things I have to do.'

As soon as she said that she compressed her lips, and her expression grew a little irritated as if she had told me more than she wanted to. Or perhaps it was the strain of speaking to me on equal terms.

She hadn't looked at Roy and he sat on the chair nearest the door, as if setting himself apart.

Baker brought us both whisky without asking. It was in big round glasses which he'd filled with ice cubes. I put mine on the floor without tasting it.

'We'll wait till Winston leaves,' I said. 'Then we'll go in and get Virginia.'

'Suppose she's not there?' Tess said.

'Then we'll just have to think again,' I said. 'Besides, we haven't actually got any evidence to suppose that he won't keep his end of the bargain. What we're doing is just insurance. If he's convinced that you won't go to the police there's really no reason for him not to let her go.'

'Even if he lets her go he can crop up again. Not exactly a thrilling prospect.'

She glanced at Baker, then at Roy, her gaze passing over him quickly as if he were an object, like the chair.

'We'll manage,' Baker said. 'The important thing is to get tonight over with.'

Tess didn't reply and I had a hunch she had a lot of other things on her mind.

'If we find her,' I said, 'we'll bring her back and ring you, so you can get out of there. If and when he rings you again you can tell him to get lost. He can hardly go around telling anyone anything without incriminating himself, and if he blows his big deal he'll have enough trouble on his plate. He'll probably disappear back up North.'

I didn't think it would be all that easy, but it sounded plausible. I looked at Roy. He was looking out of the front window with his chin propped up on his hand, giving no sign that he'd heard.

'What makes you so certain?' Baker asked.

I told him about my idea that the deal would be next day. If Winston didn't come up with the money, Goonay's associates wouldn't be pleased and his best shot would be to make himself scarce.

Baker nodded thoughtfully. Tess didn't comment. She was staring at Baker with an intensity which I felt concealed anger.

'Nice people,' she said. 'If our daughter wasn't involved I'd find it truly fascinating.'

She said this last bit with her teeth gritted, and Baker looked away from her staring eyes, his face suddenly flushing bright red.

Obviously she blamed Baker for everything that had happened. I felt a sneaking sympathy for him. When she'd stared at him

169

there was a tension in the air between them that was curiously threatening.

She stood abruptly, her eyes still on Baker, and said that she had things to do. Then she walked out of the room, looking straight ahead.

The atmosphere lightened. Baker walked towards Roy and sat on the arm of the sofa near him. Roy turned slightly, his chin still on his hand, and looked at him sideways. His face was expressionless.

'How would you like to go to college in the States?'

Roy looked flabbergasted and disbelieving. I was startled for a moment, then I felt a grudging admiration for the speed and directness with which Baker had moved to solve the problem.

It was best to get Roy out of the way before he could get into trouble or make mischief, and it had to be an offer which looked like something more than a handout, something with the promise of a future.

Above all the timing was right. Now whatever happened to Winston, Roy would know there was a way out for him.

Baker was smiling slightly, in control, as if putting a proposition to an associate, and when Roy said nothing he went on smoothly. 'Yes. It would be easier for you. Everyone does some kind of study over there. You wouldn't need to be a scholar. No one would know anything about your trouble, and it would be fun. You could study whatever you liked at whatever level you're ready for and come back after you had some qualifications. Or you could just use it as some time to decide what you wanted to do. Knock around a bit.'

Roy laughed contemptuously. 'You must be joking. They don't take fucking cons.'

'That doesn't make it impossible,' Baker said. 'Just a little more difficult. It can be fixed.'

'You can do that?'

Baker nodded slowly. He never took his eyes off Roy, who returned his gaze steadily.

'Great way to get rid of me.' Roy laughed again, a harsh, sneering sound.

'That would be easy,' Baker said. 'But I promise you that's not how it is. I don't know what kind of guarantee I can give you, and I understand you not trusting me, but we can work something out. I promise you though, that I care about you. I care about your future and that's not going to change.'

He sounded very sincere.

'It's a bit late,' Roy said. He sounded sad, rather than angry.

I glanced at Baker, but his eyes were glued to Roy's face. I wondered whether I should get up and leave. Somehow it was like being at a play, but a play which wasn't meant for spectators.

'I know,' Baker said. 'But I can't do anything about that now. Let's think about the future.'

Roy shifted a little so that he was looking out of the window again. He didn't answer.

'Think about it,' Baker said softly. 'That's all I want you to do. Think about it.'

Roy didn't move. Baker looked round at me and got up.

'Another drink?'

I shook my head. I had only sipped the first one, but I'd had enough. Being in that house with them embarrassed me and made me uneasy.

It wasn't merely the fact that their emotions were on show. That was only part of what was going on.

Both of them, I could see now, were in their different ways, skilled manipulators. Roy had tried to blackmail and rob Baker, and I was sure that when the dust settled he would start figuring out how to collect whatever he felt was due to him.

I was equally sure that Baker understood the danger. His response was to cut the ground from under Roy's feet by making the offer of a future he couldn't refuse. And all this was tied up with the resentment and longing they felt for each other.

But whatever deal they were making had nothing to do with what I'd felt about Roy. Now all I wanted was to find Virginia and get out of it.

'It's about time we went,' I told Baker. 'I'll let you know as soon as we get a result.'

Roy followed me out to the car, and I couldn't tell what happened between him and Baker because I didn't look back.

Chapter 31

Winston's car was still in the same place. The house with the board in front of it hadn't changed either, the windows staring blankly back at us.

Roy had turned out to be pretty skilful with my electronic game and he seemed to be running up a record score. Watching someone else manipulate the little stick man increased my sympathy for him.

'Go on mate,' I kept muttering. 'Go on.'

About an hour after it got dark Winston came out of the house and strolled down the pavement to his car. He didn't seem to be in a hurry.

'We'd better wait a bit,' I said. 'Make sure he's not coming back.'

Roy grunted and went back to the game.

I wondered how long it would take for Winston to get where he was going. All of a sudden the entire plan seemed impracticable. So many different things could go wrong, and we only had two hours before midnight. I couldn't wait any longer.

'Let's go,' I told Roy.

There was no doorbell, so I knocked on the door with my knuckles, then banged loudly with my fist. No answer. The house remained as dark and lifeless as ever. The memory of finding Virginia's flatmates not far from the same spot kept on coming back to me, and I felt a chill of fear at the thought that we'd find Virginia stretched out in that same state of cold pallor.

I kicked at the door. Still no answer. A passing couple looked at us curiously, then looked straight ahead again.

'Can you open it?' I asked Roy.

'Sure.'

I expected him to pick the lock and I started getting between him and the road, but instead he gripped me round the shoulders and suddenly swung himself up to smash both his feet with the whole weight of his body behind them against the lock. The door sprang open with a crash.

'It's open,' Roy said.

I looked around. No one seemed to have noticed anything, and I pushed Roy in ahead of me and closed the door behind us.

The short hallway was lined with dirty and fading wallpaper, and led to a set of uncarpeted stairs. Alongside us the doors were boarded up, and we climbed the stairs cautiously, with Roy in the lead. Suddenly a light went on above the stairs and I froze against the wall. Roy laughed and pointed to a light switch he'd just clicked on.

'All right, mate,' I said. 'We're not all experts in bloody B & E.'

The door at the top of the stairs was also locked but Roy made short work of that too, smashing it open with a speed and efficiency which impressed me. I pushed ahead of him into the flat. There were only two rooms, and there wasn't much in the way of furniture apart from a narrow single mattress on the floor of the room facing on to the back. It took only a few seconds to work out that Virginia wasn't there.

I walked back down the stairs dejectedly. Behind me I could hear Roy's footsteps echoing. Hoping against hope I tried the boarded-up doors as we went down, but it was obvious that none of them had been touched for months.

In the car we looked at each other. I was hoping that Roy would come up with something before I had to make the obvious suggestion.

'Rodney might know something,' I said slowly.

'He wouldn't tell us if he did.'

'Maybe but we've got to try something.'

'I'd try Hazel first,' he said. 'She must have seen something. Anyway she should know what's going on. That's her business.'

'She won't be out yet, though,' I said. 'We don't even know where she lives.'

'We know the estate. Let's go.'

I drove fast into Harrow Road. On the way Roy insisted on stopping and buying a takeaway Chinese meal. He said it would help us with Hazel and I was too shattered to argue. When we pulled up next to the estate where we'd seen Rodney drop her off, he got out quickly and walked straight up the walkway we'd seen her use. I followed him, content to be towed along.

He rang the bell on the first door we came to, and as the door began to open he waved me back out of sight.

'Takeaway,' he said.

'Not here,' someone said. 'But you can leave it.'

Roy laughed easily. 'No. It's a lady named Hazel. You know her?'

'No.'

The door closed. Roy looked round at me and spread his hands, then walked on to the next flight of stairs.

We worked our way up the next two floors like this, and we were ten flights up before someone pointed to another flat down the corridor.

'Try over there. Thirty-six. She's named Hazel.'

We walked over to thirty-six. There was a light on in the hall-way and Roy looked at me with his eyebrows raised. I nodded and he raised his hand to knock, then he lowered it again.

'When we're in there,' he muttered. 'If I crack on like I'm a nutter, you crack on like you're trying to restrain me. You know what I mean?'

I agreed without understanding and he knocked on the door.

Someone slid the chain into place and the door opened a narrow crack. Hazel looked through it.

'What do you want?'

She sounded Scottish. Not the grating Glasgow rasp, more like somewhere around Edinburgh.

'Takeaway,' Roy said, holding it up so she could see. 'It's all paid for, the bloke said Hazel. You've got to sign for it though.'

'Bloody hell,' she said. 'Some blokes send flowers. My bloke says it with spring onions, know what I mean?'

She opened the door, and we followed her into the flat. She must have been about to leave for the night's work because she was dressed in a short shiny black skirt with a low cut black sweater belted over it.

Up close she wasn't as young or as pretty as she'd seemed from a distance. Her makeup was too thick and it covered a skin which had a muddy, bumpy look about it. But she had a strong shapely body, and under the shiny material of the skirt her buttocks rolled and thrust suggestively. Perhaps it was because of the pose I'd seen her in the night before, but she gave off an aura of sexuality which was hard to ignore.

She led us into the big sitting room. The furnishings were chain-store chic with a long low coffee table covered with green tiles in the dead centre of the room. There were windows all along the far wall and below them a riot of pot plants. She turned and faced us in front of the coffee table.

'What have I got to sign then?'

In reply Roy hit her hard in the stomach. I hadn't expected that, and she had given a sort of loud grunt and collapsed before I realised what had happened. Almost without a pause he leaped past her, yanked her up by the hair and twisted her right arm behind her back, the other arm squeezing her throat.

'Roy,' I said. 'Take it easy.'

I had thought that he might try and frighten her, but he had already gone further than I had imagined.

He shook his head and frowned slightly over her shoulder.

'This is a surprise, love,' he said menacingly into Hazel's ear.

Her eyes rolled desperately as I watched, and she scrabbled helplessly with her free hand at the crook of Roy's elbow where it curved round her throat. She made a gurgling noise.

'I want to know where Virginia is. That chick that Winston had, the junkie. You know who I mean. He had her with him when Rodney gave him the flat to stay in, and she's not there now. I want to know where she is.'

He eased his arm away from her throat and Hazel drew great gasping breaths down into her lungs. Her bosom heaved and shuddered. The sweater had come off one shoulder and as I watched one of her breasts was squeezed out of the neckline, one stiff brown nipple pointing straight upwards and trembling every time she breathed.

'Tell me,' Roy said. 'Where is she?'

'I don't know. I don't know what you're on about,' Hazel gasped. 'He doesn't tell me nothing.'

Roy jerked viciously at the arm he had twisted behind her back and at the same time tightened his grip round her throat. She stretched on to the tips of her toes, her eyes rolled desperately and she began making the gurgling noises through her open mouth.

'That's it,' Roy hissed into her ear. 'My mate there doesn't like doing women over but I'm different.'

He waggled his eyebrows at me, and I realised that it was time for some restraint.

'Don't go too far, Roy.'

I made my voice sound nervous and concerned but it wasn't entirely play-acting. If she didn't talk soon he might well hurt her seriously and I was sure I couldn't go along with that. As it was, the whole scene already made me feel sick and guilty.

'Fuck off,' Roy said. 'She's going out the fucking window. That's my fucking sister they've got.'

He turned her round and rushed at the windows. One of them was half open and he pushed her through headfirst. She screamed but the sound was muffled by her being halfway out of the window. By now I really was nervous in case someone heard her.

'Roy,' I said. 'For fuck's sake.'

'Be over in a minute,' he said, looking round at me.

By some weird coincidence Hazel was bent over the window sill in the position I recognised from the previous night, with her skirt up round her waist, her legs splayed wide apart and quivering. Suddenly there was a ripping sound, the belt came away in one of Roy's hands and Hazel began to slip further over the window sill.

For a moment Roy was off balance and I realised that he couldn't hold her. In that instant I thought she'd gone, and in my panic, without thinking, I lunged and caught one of her legs around the knee.

We stood frozen, for what seemed a long time, the blood pounding in my ears; then as if sight and sound had abruptly been restored I heard Hazel screaming.

'Jesus,' Roy said.

He reached down, got a better grip on Hazel, and together we hauled her back in, and dumped her on the floor below the window.

My heart was pounding at the narrow escape, and I leaned back against the window sill, panting.

Hazel got up on her hands and knees and began scuttling away from us. Before I could speak Roy made a leap, grabbed her and hauled her up again to face the window.

'No,' she said, gabbling her words. 'No. I'll tell you. Winston sold her to Rodney.'

'Sold her?'

I wasn't sure that I'd heard her right.

'He wanted Rodney to break her in. Keep her for a bit and turn her out. Being a junkie it would have been easy. The dirty cow'd do anything for smack.'

'Where is she?' Roy hissed angrily. 'Just tell me where she is and shut your mouth.'

'Downstairs. In Carol's flat. Number twenty-eight.'

'Carol down there too?'

'No. She's on holiday with her kids. She left the key with me.'

'Give it to me.'

'It's in my bag.'

I picked up her bag which was lying on the floor next to the table and found the key. Roy held her all the while in the same pose as he had before but there was no need for it now. She had stopped resisting when she thought she was falling out of the window. Her makeup ran with tears and occasionally she caught her breath in a long sobbing inhalation.

'Anyone down there with her?'

'Two blokes. Mates of Rodney.'

Roy let her go and she collapsed slowly on to the floor.

'Find something to tie her up with,' he said.

I walked into the bedroom and picked up a pair of discarded stockings from the bed. Roy took them and tied her hands together then tied them to the leg of the sofa.

'Is she all right?' I asked him.

'She's brilliant,' he said. 'Rodney should come and find her when he misses her, which will be soon enough.'

He looked around as if hunting for something.

'We need a weapon.'

'No knives,' I said quickly.

I'd always hated knives and the thought of using one put me off almost as much as the thought of being on the receiving end.

Roy rolled his eyes in exasperation. He looked around some more, then picked up a small table and began wrenching it apart. In a moment he tossed me one of the legs. It had a good solid feel, and I hefted it in my hand feeling happier about tackling the two men downstairs.

'Let's go,' Roy said.

As we went out of the door I looked back at Hazel. She was lying with one hip thrust upwards, her skirt still up round her waist. I felt an irrational urge to arrange her in a more modest position before we left. Just then, she raised her head and looked at us, an angry glare which was somehow pathetic.

'Sorry, love,' I muttered. 'You'll be all right.'

'Fuck off,' she said.

Chapter 32

We took the lift down. On the next floor the doors opened and two women who were standing there took one look at us and stepped backwards. The doors closed. I looked at Roy and he shrugged. A glance had been enough to tell the women that they didn't want to get in with us, and I didn't blame them.

Roy was carrying his table leg over one shoulder and his eyes glittered with rage and excitement. In different circumstances I probably would have wanted to avoid getting in the lift with him myself. At that moment he looked at me and winked, and it struck me then that he could well be thinking the same thing about the way I looked.

'Hey Roy,' I said. 'Let's see if we can do this thing without killing anyone. Know what I mean?'

He held my eyes grimly. 'You can't fuck around with these guys. They're serious.'

He paused and looked away. When he looked back at me he was frowning.

'You know what they mean by breaking her in?'

I shook my head.

'They keep them on their own. No clothes. Not much food. Plenty of drink or dope if they want it, and they screw them all the time. It's like brainwashing. After that they're ready for the life.'

The doors opened and we tiptoed down to twenty-eight. Roy put his finger to his lips for silence, and eased the key gently

179

into the lock. Then he pushed the door open and we found ourselves in a hallway.

The flat was built on exactly the same pattern as Hazel's. Straight ahead we could see the sitting room. There was no one in it. To the right the bedroom door was ajar and we could hear voices and laughter.

'Ram it Rasta,' a voice said. 'I tell ya. Gwan, ram it.'

There was a series of rhythmic grunts, then a loud groan and the voice broke into a hysterical high-pitched laugh.

Roy pushed the door open slowly.

The man whose voice we had heard was sitting at the foot of the bed watching another man thrusting away between Virginia's outspread thighs.

From where we stood we could see her face pressed against the pillow. It had no expression, and she looked comatose, inert.

The reflection in the dressing table mirror made the whole room seem full of naked bodies, and for an instant my eyes focused on the completely bald head of the man hanging over her, gleaming with sweat and nodding vigorously as he pumped himself into her.

Roy took a fast step into the room and swung his club like an axe at the seated man's skull. But there must have been a flicker of movement on the edge of his vision because he shied away and flung his arm up to protect his head. He got the full crunching force of the blow on his forearm and went over against the wall. As he fell Roy was on him, kicking him about the ribs and stomach so hard and fast that half a dozen blows must have hit before I could shout at him to stop it.

All this had happened so quickly that the man on top of Virginia had only had a chance to turn his head. Now he began to lever himself cautiously away from her.

Roy turned away from his first victim and slashed the club across backhanded. It connected with a horrible clunking sound and the man fell across Virginia, writhing. Roy reached down and heaved him off the bed.

'Get her clothes,' he ground out from between his teeth.

He got on to the bed beside Virginia and lifted her. She lolled limply into his arms, not moving or making a sound. I opened the wardrobe and took out a dressing gown I found there.

Together we draped it round her and forced her hands down the sleeves. She still hadn't moved and she didn't seem capable of walking.

'Carry her,' Roy said.

He slung her over my shoulders in a fireman's lift. She felt light and frail. I could feel her hipbones against my neck muscles.

'What are you going to carry?' I asked Roy.

'Any bugger gives us trouble,' he said, hefting his club. 'I'll deal with them. You want to change places?'

I shook my head.

'Then bloody go.'

One of the men on the floor groaned and moved, and Roy turned and kicked out with all his force, as if he was booting a football.

'Cut it out for Christ's sake,' I shouted.

He glared at me, then, with a conscious effort calmed himself down.

'Okay,' he said irritably. 'Get on with it.'

He reached the door before I did and peered round it into the corridor.

'Come on,' he said. 'Let's take the stairs.'

When we got to the car I dumped Virginia into the back with relief. It wasn't her weight so much as the prospect that someone would by now have called the police, and we'd be stopped. Once in the car I felt safer.

Roy got in the other side, belted himself in and gestured at me.

'Not too fast, eh.'

I drove at a moderate clip up towards the river. Going round Hyde Park Corner Virginia gave a moaning sound but when I looked back she still seemed to be spark out in the back. I had thought her thin before. Now she was skeletal, with big blue smudges under her eyes.

'Think she'll be all right?'

Roy shrugged. 'I don't know.'

I looked back at her and wondered once again how and why someone like her had got into this state. Baker was father to these two and maybe that said something about him.

The interplay between Tess and her husband every time I'd

181

seen them together had told me more about his insecurity and dependence on her than I could have imagined, and I wondered how he'd handle all the combined problems that his wife and children would provide.

One thing was certain. When I first met him I thought that he had it made, now I wouldn't be in his shoes for anything.

The man himself opened the door as we drew up in front of his house. He came across the pavement hurriedly, and scooped Virginia out of the car without a word. Then he carried her in, while we walked behind like mourners at a funeral. Inside the door he looked round at me.

'What's the matter with her?'

'She's probably high on something,' I said. 'But I'd get a doctor.'

He turned and mounted the stairs two at a time. Roy walked into the sitting room and when I followed him in he was pouring himself a drink.

'Want some?'

I shook my head. I didn't know what I wanted.

'Well,' he said. 'I'm owed this much at least.' He laughed angrily.

'More than that,' I told him.

Baker came back into the room, walked to the phone and dialled. Someone came on the other end and he told them there'd been an accident. His daughter needed attention right away.

'Good job your doc's private,' Roy said.

His tone was sneering and aggressive. Baker shot him an angry glance and he was about to say something when I interrupted.

'You'd better phone your wife. It's gone eleven.'

He picked the phone up and dialled again. Tess must have answered it because he told her Virginia was home. He asked her how she was.

'You'd better leave now,' he said.

I couldn't tell what she said in reply, but his hand tightened on the receiver and he made a frustrated angry gesture with it.

'We agreed,' he said. 'You ought to leave now.'

182

Suddenly he stopped, took the phone away from his ear, put it back and began to say his wife's name loudly.

'Hello,' he shouted. 'Tess, answer me. Hello.'

He put it down and turned round.

'She's been cut off.'

'Try it again,' I said.

He dialled and listened. He held the phone out to me. I put it to my ear and heard it ringing but there was no answer.

'Something's wrong,' he said.

He stared at me for a moment, but I had the feeling he was looking straight through me at the wall.

'I'm going down there,' he said.

'What about Virginia? You can't leave her right now.'

'I'll go,' Roy said.

I laughed with genuine amusement. Winston, Roy, and Tess all together sounded like a recipe for disaster.

'I'll go,' I said.

I didn't want to, but somehow I couldn't leave it alone. I had to see the whole thing through to the end.

'Lend me your car,' I said.

Baker's big BMW was just the thing for the motorway. He handed me the keys without a word. I looked at my watch.

'It's nearly half past eleven,' I said. 'If you don't hear from me by one thirty you'd better call the cops.'

'Wait a minute,' he said.

He was scribbling on a piece of paper, and he handed it to me. It had the number of the turnoff and a crude diagram, with the name of the village and on the other side the address of the house.

Roy followed me to the door.

'You stay with him,' I said. 'By the time I get there whatever's happening will have happened.'

He looked at me with a mournful expression as if I was breaking up the good old team, but I was certain that he would only complicate the situation, whatever it was, when I got there.

'I can handle it,' he said.

'Use your head,' I told him. 'We don't know what the hell is happening, and we only just got Virginia back. If Winston or Rodney or anyone else shows up, somebody should be with him.'

183

I jerked my head towards the sitting room. I didn't believe there was any chance whatsoever of that happening, but while he was thinking about it I slipped through the front door and closed it firmly behind me.

Chapter 33

The car had a solid, cushioned feel about it, and it took the bends with a sure grip that made me want to go faster.

The next time I looked at my watch I was on the motorway and halfway to Watford Junction. It felt good to be moving out into the country, but when I looked up at the sky I could see dark clouds on the horizon to the north. The road seemed to be carrying me straight towards them.

I had turned on the radio and got a pirate station which played dub, but as I cleared London, the signal faded and I got the arts programme on the World Service. I turned it up louder so that the speakers at the back blasted out the carefully cultivated enthusiasm of the voices; and there was something comfortably surreal about belting along the motorway listening to them talking about Pavarotti.

The turnoff came sooner than I expected and I took it too fast. The car canted and skidded dangerously. I went down to third and back up again without a pause, my hands and feet moving automatically. I shook my head. There'd been something hypnotic about the motorway and the sound of the radio. On the narrower, twisting road I began to wake up.

I hadn't thought about what I would find when I got there but I had the feeling that I didn't really care what happened to either of them.

At the same time my mind played over fantasies of death and

destruction, a burning house, Tess crawling down the middle of the roadway, a trail of blood behind her.

The village was wrapped in sleeping darkness and I slowed down to navigate my way through it, but it was really only a cluster of houses around the road. Through the houses the road split and I took the left hand fork as Baker's map directed.

A few hundred yards on I saw the house. It stood on its own with a ploughed field on one side and a small copse of trees on the other.

Opposite was another field. A low brick wall ran right around the big garden. Over it I could just see the lighted windows on the ground floor, and immediately afterwards I registered the sight of a big black car with its lights off parked close by the wall.

I drove on past the open gate and pulled on to the grass verge about fifty yards down. When I opened the door and got out the silence hit me. There were some animal noises, a dog barking in the distance, some sort of birds chirping and hooting occasionally, but apart from that, no sound, not even traffic.

It was a curious sensation for an ear tuned to the human voices and mechanical sounds of the city.

As I eased my way through the gate a light went on in one of the upstairs windows and a shadow crossed it. A moment later another shadow moved across and another light went on in what looked like a bathroom window.

I stood inside the gate trying to figure it out. If those two shadows were Tess and Winston they'd been upstairs in the dark, and what that meant I didn't dare to think. Another light went on and I saw someone coming down the stairs through the frosted glass of the transom window at the top of the door.

I looked at the curtained windows trying to find a crack I could peer through to suss the situation, and I tiptoed towards the house as I did so.

Suddenly there was a loud bang.

For a moment I thought it might have come from the road and I looked around sharply. As it died away I realised it had to have come from the house. I froze, then started going for the door, but that instant of indecision had given me time to identify the sound and think about it.

The sound had been a gunshot and behind that door would be someone with a gun who had no inhibitions about shooting it off. I dithered for another second, and I had just made up my mind to go for the door when someone opened up a narrow gap in the curtains and peeped through.

I was out of their line of sight along the drive and through the gate and I stood as still as a statue. The curtains closed again, leaving a fine space through which the light gleamed like a beacon. I crept towards it and looked through cautiously.

Tess was standing there with the telephone in her hand. It was one of those small ones with the dial set in the middle, and as I watched she dialled three times. She was stark naked, with a blue dress clutched firmly under one arm.

I turned my head and saw a pair of denim trousered legs stretched out on the floor. I kept craning my head to see but my vision couldn't go any further than the man's shoulders. He was lying face down, but I didn't need to see any more, because his huge frame told me it was Winston, and the blood seeping rapidly from under his chest told me he was either dead or well on the way to it.

A flicker of movement caught my eye. Tess had the dress between her hands and she tore it fiercely, then she slipped it over her head and picked up the phone again. She dialled and began to speak.

She looked excited and she gestured forcefully, wagging her finger as if she was talking to a person who was standing in front of her.

I peered around looking for the briefcase, but I couldn't see it. My eyes came back as if drawn to Winston's body. He hadn't moved, and I wondered if there was a chance that he was still alive.

The picture came to my mind, unbidden, of the two of us driving through Hampstead, one behind the other. The poor bastard would never dream of millions again.

I looked for the gun and saw it lying just beyond the body, its snout almost touching him like a finger pointing to the damage.

Tess put the phone down and walked out of sight and I began edging my way towards the door, wondering whether to knock or just try it to see if it was open. On the way I kept seeing nasty pictures of Tess blasting away with the shotgun as I stepped inside.

At the back of my mind was some vague idea about seeing

whether Winston was really dead and whether I could help him, but I also had the feeling that if I squeezed my eyes shut and shook my head the picture of the body stretched out on the floor in its own blood would disappear.

I had just put out my hand to try the door knob when I heard the sirens in the distance.

As if by reflex I turned and started to run, crashing through the garden and over the wall in the time it took me to think the action. I hadn't locked the car and I was in motion, still struggling into my seat belt, by the time the first police car came round the bend behind me.

I kept on going, forcing myself to keep a nice steady pace, my guts twisting round the idea that they would chase me down. Instead the car screeched into the gateway of the house.

Behind it I could see the flashing lights of the ambulance.

I took the first turning and found myself going back through the village. I drove about a mile up the road and stopped at the first phone booth. Baker answered on the first ring.

'Where are you?' he said.

I guessed that Tess must have rung and told him that I'd never arrived. I wondered whether he'd explain what had happened.

'I've only just reached the village,' I said. 'I got lost. I'll be there in five minutes if I'm on the right road.'

'Don't,' he said urgently. 'Come back. Don't go near the house.'

'Why not?' I said innocently. 'Have you heard? Is it all right?'

There was a brief pause.

'There's been an accident,' he said. 'He attacked her and she had to shoot him.'

'Shoot him? Is he dead?'

'Yes. Yes,' he said impatiently. 'I don't want to talk about this on the phone. The best thing is for you to come straight back. There's no point in your being involved.'

'Doesn't she need some help?'

'Our solicitor will be there by now,' he said. 'You can't help. It's better if you don't get involved for your own sake.'

As hell as like, I thought. I said nothing, just listened to his rapid breathing.

'You needn't bring the car back immediately,' he said. 'Keep it till tomorrow. Bring it round then. If we're not in you can stick the keys through the door.'

'All right,' I said.

He put the phone down and I listened to its high-pitched whine for a few seconds. I looked at my hands. They weren't trembling but everything seemed to take a very long time, like putting the phone down and getting out of the phone booth and into the car again. When I'd made it I turned the heater up and drove.

Halfway back I stopped at a motorway café for a cup of coffee and as soon as I'd drunk it I went into the gents and vomited up everything in my stomach. Afterwards I went back for another cup, and huddled into the red plastic seat drinking it slowly.

I stayed there until dawn rose pink in the sky. Then I drove slowly back to London.

Chapter 34

I woke up at about two in the afternoon. I'd had one of those nightmares in which I was paralysed and couldn't move while some nameless threat hung over me.

When I'd woken from it, sweating and tormented, my first impulse was to check the flat to see whether anyone had broken in, but I couldn't move or do anything except moan feebly, and I'd slipped gradually back into unconsciousness, resigned to whatever happened.

I got out of bed and began remembering the night before. Up to the point where I saw Winston lying on the floor it was hard to imagine that I would care what happened to him, but now I felt a kind of grief and anger it was equally hard to explain.

Some of it was to do with Roy, I thought, because in a way he had been telling me that Winston was part of him and whatever else happened, I knew his friend's death would hurt him. But it was more than that.

Over the last few days I had begun to understand the sense in which Winston, with his incoherent fury, violence, and muddled ambition, was part of what I was too, and he'd lost his life chasing a dream which had lured too many people I knew into darkness and death.

I rang Baker. No reply. I waited and tried again. Still nothing.

After the third time I rang his office, and got the answering service. I left a message saying I wanted to know what to do with the car.

I rang Pete. A machine answered. I said I didn't know what to do with the car and asked whether I should take it to the police. I added that I might have to do that if I didn't hear from anyone.

I looked out the window at the big BMW. The shops were closed, and standing by itself at a row of meters, it had a bold rich look, as if it were signalling the kind of invulnerability that went with wealth.

An Arab man followed by two women with masks on walked slowly past. At the junction he stopped and began looking around, uncertain about the name of the street. Then he made his decision and turned left, the women waddling awkwardly after him.

I watched them till they were out of sight, dreaming.

When the phone rang it jerked me out of a reverie that was like sleep. I picked it up and heard Pete's voice.

'Hey, Sammy,' he said. 'I got your message about the car. That's great. I'll come and pick it up.'

'No. You bloody won't,' I said. 'I want to talk to the Bakers. Understand? You're the oily rag, mate.'

There was a silence. In the background I could hear the noise of children calling out.

'They won't see you, Sammy. You've done a great job. They're very grateful, but it's all over. They've got everything under control.'

'You know what happened last night?'

Pete's voice was hushed but it sounded smug under the concern.

'I know,' he said. 'Look. I shouldn't tell you this but I think you have a right to know why they're so upset. If any stories come out they'll mention Mrs B and they'll say she was attacked by an intruder and used the shotgun in self-defence. They won't mention it, but she was raped you know. The guy was an animal. It's open and shut, and in the present law and order climate it shouldn't create any difficulty.'

'Were you there, Pete?'

'What do you mean?'

'I said were you bloody well there?'

I shut my eyes. It was probably the effect of the sunlight but it seemed as if a red rage was boiling behind them.

'He had it coming, Sammy.'

191

'That's how you folks arrange the world. You're always right.'

'Look, Sam. I'll come and pick up the car in an hour or so.'

'No. You look, Pete. Get Tess and tell her I know about the dress. Tell her I got there early. I heard the shot and I was looking through the window. Tell her that and I think she'll want to see me.'

A tight band seemed to be squeezing my chest and I breathed with difficulty. I folded my arms in front of me, holding myself together.

'All right, Sammy.'

He put the phone down immediately.

I lay on the bed until I'd calmed down. It was obvious that Tess had sold her story to everyone who mattered. The thoughts charged around my head. I hated them all.

The phone rang suddenly, making me jump with surprise.

'You wanted to talk to me?' she asked, when I didn't speak.

'Yes. Pete told you what I said?'

'Yes. But I'm not sure why it should concern me.'

'Keep this up and I'll take the car down the nearest nick and let them sort it out.'

There was a brief pause.

'Why don't you bring it round now? I'll be at home for a while.'

Within half an hour I was driving over Chelsea Bridge. It was another bright day and Battersea Park looked beautiful in the sunshine of the late morning. The night before had been damp and there was still enough moisture in the atmosphere to make everything sparkle.

It was on mornings like these, the medieval poets wrote, that knights went forth to do battle with dragons and rescue beautiful maidens with golden hair.

Tess had golden hair, but if my guess was right she was also the next best thing to a dragon. She had killed Winston. No dispute. But if I'd read the situation right, it certainly wasn't in self-defence.

I wasn't sure how she'd accounted for being there on her own or how she'd set up the breaking and entering scenario, but I was sure that her story would have been air-tight. Rape would add the final touch of credibility and with Winston dead there was no one around to contradict her.

192

Except for me; and I didn't know myself why I was going to confront her. In spite of my threats I couldn't believe that whatever it was I thought I'd seen would make a difference. But I was thinking of Roy.

I had seriously underestimated Tess, and if she felt about him the way I thought she did, I ought to make sure that he was safe, and perhaps help him find some way out of the situation, before her hostility destroyed him, or maybe it was just that I had to know for certain.

When I rang the bell Pete answered. He gave me a small tight smile.

'Where's Roy?' I said.

'He's fine. He's on holiday with Baker.'

'Don't bullshit me, Pete. I'm not in the mood.'

He looked hurt.

'I'm not. Come in.'

He retreated into the hallway. I followed him and the door swung shut behind me. There was no sign of Tess.

'They've come to an arrangement. Honestly. They're spending a week together, and they'll discuss what Roy will do with his life. Baker's really taking this seriously, spending time on getting it right.'

I smiled at the politician's phrase.

'You're kidding me.'

'I kid you not,' Pete said. He lowered his voice.

'Baker's no fool. He's told the people who matter, and the signs are that if he can hold his family life together, and be discreet about Roy, no one will feel that it's any of their business. It all happened a long time ago, you see, when he was an impressionable young man. If he accepts his responsibilities and manages sensibly, it won't do him any harm to speak of.'

So it had all been arranged.

'What about Roy?'

'Oh well. Roy. If he can go away and study something for a while, then come back with his past behind him he should do very nicely. They're talking about that now, and he'll have lots of support. Next time you see Roy you won't know him.'

He laughed.

'He's accepted all this?'

Pete spread his hands and shrugged, raising his eyebrows.

'I've got the telephone number of the place in Scotland for you. Don't take my word for it. You can ring and speak to him.'

He gave me a plain card with the phone number written on it in black ink. It looked elegant.

'Will that do?' Pete said. 'Or do you still want to see Tess?'

He had regained his assurance, as if he could see I was shaken, and his tone was quizzical.

'Yes. I want to see her.'

Without a word he turned, and led the way into the kitchen. Tess was sitting at the table as he opened the door, looking at us expressionlessly.

I sat down opposite her. Pete lounged against the open door.

I looked at him.

'Amscray, Pete.'

He shook his head.

'Nogoro.'

His schoolgirl sister had taught us this kids' gibberish one weekend many years ago. Gazing at him now I wondered where she was.

I looked at Tess.

'You really don't want him here while we're talking,' I said.

Pete broke in before she could reply.

'If you're going to make wild accusations,' he said quickly, 'I want to be here. Remember I brought you here because we were friends and I trusted you. It's all over and it's about time you recognised that.'

I ignored him and kept my eyes on Tess.

'Yes or no,' I said.

'I'll ring you later, Pete,' she said. She looked at him with the same blank serious face she had for me.

'Are you sure?' he said anxiously.

Her face puckered into a grimace that was supposed to be a smile.

'I'll be all right,' she said.

'If you're sure,' he said.

'I'll take a nap in a little while,' she said, 'and when I wake I'll ring you. Thanks for looking after me.'

She said this with a little girl sweetness that was almost touching. Pete walked over, bent, and kissed her cheek, very close to her mouth.

I raised my eyebrows and he straightened up, glaring at me. Then he marched stiffly to the door and went out without looking back.

'Pete's getting pompous in his old age,' I said.

She gave me a sly little smile in reply.

'You're really a woman of mystery,' I told her.

'Say what you've come to say,' she said sharply. 'I'm tired and I've had a difficult time. I'd like to get this over with as quickly as possible.'

I told her about going down to the house and what I'd seen through the curtains.

She sat looking at her hands, loosely clasped on the table in front of her, and she didn't move, except when I got to the part about seeing the shadows behind the windows upstairs, and then she looked up and stared straight at me.

'You didn't look like a woman in a state of alarm,' I said. 'Nothing like it.'

She smiled. 'Why didn't you go to the police with all this? You could have just waited for them to arrive and told them your story.'

The truth was I had panicked.

'I'm thinking about it,' I said. 'I can still do that, but I need to know what happened. Why did you do it?'

'There'll be an inquest soon. Perhaps you'd like to give your testimony.'

She was watching me carefully, like a cat. Something about her look made me feel she was probing for weaknesses and I almost shuddered, remembering the body and the blood and her cool abstracted air as she stood at the telephone.

'There's Roy,' I said, 'and Virginia, and Baker.'

'Virginia's ill,' she said. 'At about this moment,' she glanced at her watch, 'she's on her way to a secure clinic in Geneva. My husband and Roy are tramping about the mud in Scotland, and soon they'll be in the USA. It's time poor Roy found somewhere he can settle.'

Her hypocrisy was breathtaking. She smiled broadly.

'I think you'll find,' she said, 'that Roy has accepted the facts with good grace, and I think you'll also find that he knows on which side his bread is buttered. We'll manage Roy.'

'What about your husband?' I said. 'He's got a conscience.'

195

She smiled that smile again.

'Do you know how naive you sound?' She sounded almost playful. 'He knows what he needs to know.'

'And little naive me. What about me?'

'Oh come along. Surely there's something you want?'

'Whatever it is, it's got blood on it.'

The smile disappeared and she looked angry for the first time. 'Don't talk to me about blood,' she said. 'That animal deserved whatever he got. He kidnapped my daughter, filled her full of drugs, tried to turn her into a prostitute and you talk to me about blood. If he'd had any sense and he hadn't been a vicious bully he'd still be alive.'

Her voice had taken on a hectoring schoolmarmish note, and she glared at me across the table.

'But he didn't attack you,' I said. 'I saw you tear that dress and you practically had a smile on your face when you picked up the phone.'

She smiled broadly again, but this time her eyes bulged and she showed her teeth with a grinning fixity that alarmed me.

'No. He didn't. But he was so stupid that it didn't occur to him that I might have anything on my mind besides sex, and he didn't need much encouragement to jump on me. He was very stupid. Not frightening at all. More annoying, as a matter of fact. When we came downstairs and I picked up the gun, he laughed.'

She looked away from me, and her voice took on a quiet reflective quality as if she was talking to herself.

'I wanted to shoot him when I went down there. That's why I loaded the gun. But I don't think I could have gone through with it if he hadn't done the things he did.'

'But why?' I asked her numbly. 'You can spare the money.'

'It wasn't the money,' she said fiercely. 'If you want the truth, I loathed him. He made my flesh crawl and the thought of what he'd done to my daughter sickened me. Sickened me. He was an animal. I've got horses more human than that.'

'You're crazy,' I said involuntarily. 'Nuts.'

Her face now was a grinning red and white mask, and I didn't think she'd heard me. Then she started again, quietly, but speaking with an intensity that was ferocious.

'You're so clever,' she said. 'Who do you think you're talking to? Who do you think you are? You're exactly the same kind of scum. And my husband had a child with one of you. When he told me I was sick for days. I couldn't eat for disgust.'

'You ought to see a doctor,' I said. 'You're well round the bend.'

She didn't move, simply kept on staring with the same crazy grin. Suddenly I wanted to strike back, lash her with words that would hurt.

'It's bullshit,' I shouted. 'You can comfort yourself with that race hatred crap, but you're sicker than you know. You knew very well what your daughter was getting plenty of and you wanted some.'

In my rage I stood up and came closer, pointing at her.

'And you got it too, didn't you? Even though you had to kill the guy afterwards to cover up. You won't forget that. What are you going to do next time? There's got to be a next time, 'cause you loved that animal fucking you, didn't you? You loved it.'

She came at me then. I hadn't noticed the bread knife on the table, and when she got up and lunged at me it was in her hand. She wasn't Rodney though, and I saw it coming before she swung it at me. I parried it with my left hand and smashed her full in the face with my right. She sat down on the floor abruptly and began to wail. In between the fingers she had clutched over her face I could see blood flowing.

'Oh shit,' I said. 'This is pointless.'

I looked around and spotted a roll of kitchen paper. I gave it to her.

'Hold your head back,' I said.

We sat like that for a couple of minutes while she snuffled and dabbed at her nose with handfuls of paper. Sitting opposite me, with her head leaning back, a bunch of sodden bits of paper clutched in front of her face, she looked pathetic.

'None of this matters,' she said. 'It might be troublesome if you went around telling your story but in the end it would be ignored or it would be hushed up. Roy and Virginia would be the ones to suffer.'

She paused. She stared at me over the mask of bloody tissues.

'And you, of course. You don't know how hard things could be for you.'

I had an inkling.

197

'That sounds like a stalemate,' I said. 'But if I keep my mouth shut, what are you going to do?'

She thought for a little while.

'How much do you want?'

'I don't want your money,' I said. 'I don't like you. Taking it would make me feel bad. I'm thinking about Roy. I want you to promise you won't hurt him or make things more difficult than they need to be.'

It was odd, after all that had been said in that room, asking this woman to promise. Even odder was my sense that if she made the promise she would keep it.

She lowered her head a little to look at me.

'Yes. I'll do what I can.'

'Just don't mess him about.'

She nodded impatiently. Looking at her, I wished that it wasn't true that Roy had fallen in with them so easily. But he had always been a lost boy, and this was the nearest thing to home that he'd find.

'You haven't got away with it,' I said. 'I might not be able to do anything, but I know.'

'I thought it was a bargain,' she said.

'I can't bargain over other people's lives. I'm just trying for the best deal I can get.'

She glared at me but she didn't speak.

I got up and walked to the door. I looked back, but she hadn't moved and she was staring straight at the wall. She still looked pathetic with her hands cradling her face, but I felt glad I had hit her because for a little while I had begun to think about her as extraordinarily malevolent and evil.

Now she seemed only an ordinary person, curdled and corrupted by circumstances she couldn't control, and passions she didn't know how to live with. I'd probably go past hundreds like her on the way home.

'Don't you mind what you did?' I asked.

She looked up at me, then away again, her eyes dull and unseeing. She made a sound I didn't understand.

'What?'

She shook her head in reply. I stood there for a bit, but she didn't speak or look up, so I shrugged and went out of the door. That had to be the end of it.

My car felt different after Baker's, but being in it once more was comforting, like coming home. As I strapped on the seat belt I remembered that the last time I'd been in it had been with Roy, and I wondered what would become of him in this nest of snakes.

I had a hunch, though, that the rage and bitterness he had suffered, would fuel a ruthlessness as deep as Tess Baker's.

The thought made me sad, but there was nothing more to be done. I turned the key in the ignition, and the car started immediately, so I put it into gear and drove away.

Riding the Iron Rooster Paul Theroux

An eye-opening and entertaining account of travels in old and new China, from the author of *The Great Railway Bazaar*. 'Mr Theroux cannot write badly ... in the course of a year there was almost no train in the vast Chinese rail network on which he did not travel' – Ludovic Kennedy

Touched by Angels Derek Jameson

His greatest story yet – his own. 'My story is simple enough. I grew up poor and hungry on the streets of London's East End and decided at an early age it was better to be rich and successful.'

The Rich are Different Susan Howatch

Wealth is power – and all power corrupts. 'A superb saga, with all the bestselling ingredients – love, hate, death, murder, and a hell of a lot of passion' – *Daily Mirror*

The Cold Moons Aeron Clement

For a hundred generations the badgers of Cilgwyn had lived in harmony with nature – until a dying stranger limped into their midst, warning of the coming of men. Men whose scent had inexplicably terrified him, men armed with rifles and poison gas...

The Return of Heroic Failures Stephen Pile

The runaway success of *The Book of Heroic Failures* was a severe embarrassment to its author. From the song-free Korean version of *The Sound of Music* to the least successful attempt to tranquillize an animal, his hilarious sequel plumbs new depths of human incompetence.